God Bless

David E. Plant

Lorraine M. Pla

Jack Mann Phil

Smith & Priest

Kébec Series, Book 2

David E. Plante *with* Lorraine M. Plante

CROSSBOOKS
PUBLISHING

CrossBooks™
A Division of LifeWay
1663 Liberty Drive
Bloomington, IN 47403
www.crossbooks.com
Phone: 1-866-879-0502

First published by CrossBooks 1/3/2013

ISBN: 978-1-4627-2405-5 (sc)
ISBN: 978-1-4627-2407-9 (hc)
ISBN: 978-1-4627-2406-2 (e)
Library of Congress Control Number: 2012924023

Interior Graphics/Art Credit Courtesy of Jack Mann

Printed in the United States of America

This book is printed on acid-free paper.

*Any people depicted in stock imagery provided by Thinkstock are models,
and such images are being used for illustrative purposes only.*

Certain stock imagery © Thinkstock.

Contents

Also by

DAVID E. PLANTE with LORRAINE M. PLANTE

ABENAKI VALLEY

Kébec Series, Book 1
David E. Plante with
Lorraine M. Plante

Lorraine and I dedicate this book to the memory of our beloved son,

CHRISTOPHER ANTHONY PLANTE,

September 24, 1963 – January 2, 2005.

Fourth generation military.

Chris, a corporal in the U.S. Marine Corps, served to protect the freedoms of our country. We honor his service.

Acknowledgments

Many deserved thanks to everyone at CrossBooks who shared their expertise and made the publishing of *Priest & Smith* possible.

A special thanks to Jack Mann for the pictures he created and provided for this book. He and his wife, Evelyn, are the owners of Brant Apple Farm in Brant, New York. His pictures can be accessed at www.brantapplefarm.com.

Introduction

Abenaki Valley, the first book in this series, introduced Henry Priest and Zoel Smith. They were destined to become father and adopted son as well as business partners in New France in the 1600s.

Henry is an educated teacher and trained linguist. As a lifetime Bible student, he enjoys sharing with others what he has learned and does so at every opportunity the Lord provides. After satisfying his contract with the French government, he, Zoel, Josh Ink, and Yancy, an Algonquin Indian, form a trapping and fur-trading partnership and spend two years building the business.

In the process of developing the business, Henry feels led by the Holy Spirit to venture farther down the Connecticut River in search of a place to fulfill his vision to establish a mission on a large lake south of the snow-capped mountains. There, he plans to care for sick and abandoned Indians as well as share with them his knowledge of Jesus and His saving power.

Zoel continues to focus on the trapping and trading

business, which will help provide the funding to support both Henry's mission and Father Neel's and Father Donne's Quebec City mission.

This story is about the unique lives of some of the Europeans who come to the New World to discover how God plans to use their lives for good. The historic facts are quoted and noted in the References and Notes section of the book, but the biographical observations are fictional. We hope you will find His truth in the experiences of Henry and Zoel and their family and friends.

Characters

In order of appearance:

<u>Zoel Smith</u> is French by birth. At the age of twelve, his parents die aboard a ship traveling from France to New France. He is adopted by Henry Priest. He is one of four partners in a trapping and fur-trading business.

<u>Henry Priest</u> is French by birth. He is a self-educated teacher and linguist by trade. He was hired by the French government to travel to New France to learn and document Indian languages. With that assignment completed, he is now one of four partners in a trapping and fur-trading business.

<u>Josh Ink</u> is French by birth. He was one of the earliest trappers in New France. He is now one of four partners in a trapping and fur-trading business.

<u>Yancy</u> is an Algonquin Indian brave. Josh Ink saved his life when he found Yancy being attacked by two renegade warriors

during their attempted theft of a village canoe. He is one of four partners in a trapping and fur-trading business.

Father Neel and Father Donne are priests in a growing church in Quebec City.

Sooleawa (silver) is an Algonquin girl found by Yancy during the partnership's first business trip south. She had been brutalized and left for dead.

Anna (mother) is an Algonquin woman also found by Yancy during the partnership's first business trip south. She, along with her friend Sooleawa, had been brutalized and left for dead. She is now married to Henry Priest.

Etu (sun) and Ezhno (solitary) are young Abenaki council members and friends of Zoel.

Nadie (wise) is Henry and Anna's daughter who was born in midsummer. Her full name is Nadie May Priest.

Peter Smith is an English child cared for by Father Neel and Father Donne.

Chepi (fairy) is Yancy's friend in Quebec City. Now a widow, she not only works at the dress shop but also cares for her in-laws and six orphaned girls.

Adoette (big tree) is an Abenaki Indian lady from Abenaki Village One located near the Connecticut River.

Leon Durand is the horse caretaker hired by Zoel's grandfather to bring four horses to New France. He becomes a full-time employee of the joint venture.

Halona (of happy fortune) is a Pennacook Indian lady from the Pennacook village located at the beginning of the Merrimack River.

CHAPTER 1

Dad's Gift

We were beginning to talk about how it had rained every day for two weeks in Abenaki Valley just to let us know winter was over. The snow was gone, and the ice on the river had melted. But it was still cold at night, although not cold enough to freeze. We spent much of the time inside our wigwam—trying to stay positive. Henry Priest, my dad by adoption, and Anna (my mother by the same token) were looking forward to the birth of their first natural child. Anna was sick off and on—usually in the morning. I, Zoel Smith, helped with the cooking when she didn't feel well. And Henry continued to teach his French Bible classes.

The Abenaki Indians, with whom we had wintered, were ready for clear, sunny days and warmer nights. The chief and his council were planning the fur-trapping season. They knew Josh and Yancy—Henry's and my trapping and fur-trading partners—would soon be returning from Quebec City with many needed goods. Fur trapping was the first thing on many of the families' minds. The chief had asked Henry one night what he expected Josh and Yancy to bring back with them. Henry told him there would be many small, light items, such as clothes, silverware, pots and pans, knives, medicines, metal arrowheads, and jewelry.

I thought the chief had more on his mind than he disclosed when he asked Henry what his plans were for the spring and summer. Henry told him it depended on how Anna was feeling. He was anxious to head down the Connecticut River, but he was concerned about Anna's and the baby's health.

I sat in the background listening to them and the sound of the rain and realized how much the baby was going to change our lives. Would we stay here until it was born? I hoped so for Anna's sake. There were many experienced midwives in the village, and I certainly hoped Henry wouldn't try to deliver the baby all by himself in the wild.

*   *   *

The rain finally stopped, and within days everything was green and lush. It was like the sun was drawing beauty from the wet ground through the trees, bushes, flowers, and grasses. It was good to be warm and healthy again. After spending much of the winter recovering from a rattlesnake bite, I knew I would never take my health for granted again. I worked with the team of braves and replenished the wood the village had burned during both the winter and the rainy spring. Like many of the braves, I enjoyed physical labor. We had heard about two newly married couples who needed wigwams, so we volunteered to help them and their families build them. That was fun and educational.

There were a number of canoe builders in the village. They were all busy repairing winter's damage to the canoes, plus they were building new ones. I asked, "Henry, are we going to need canoes to travel down the river?"

"Yes, eventually. And when we do, we can trade for them."

We still had many things left in the supply wigwam to trade. The villagers, however, had almost no furs to trade, so I could see Henry's point. I told him I was going to learn how to build a canoe and headed off to see the canoe builder I had met just a few days earlier.

"If I help you, will you teach me how to build a canoe?" I politely asked him.

"Sure," he said as he continued working.

He was busy and didn't have a lot of help. My team of braves was off hunting, so I was able to spend most of my time learning how to build and repair canoes. Finding the ash wood to frame the canoes was the toughest part. The builder said there were only three places where ash grew. While I searched in each place for the long, slender branches he needed, others looked for birch bark to enclose the frame and for pine pitch to seal the hull.

Gathering and preparing the materials to build the canoes was a bigger job than assembling them. Shaping and tying the frames with trimmed tree roots took hand strength. The builder didn't look strong, but he certainly had powerful hands. I followed his instructions carefully as I tied ash branches together. At the end of the day, my hands really, really ached.

We had a team of at least six or seven working on canoes

every day. The results were excellent. When I got back to our wigwam at night, I used Henry's pen and paper to make notes of what I had learned about making wigwams and canoes. I thought about making a canoe for myself, but I decided Henry was right. We could trade for some in the village. I would be able to make one later if we needed it. Henry said, "I'm sure your father would be proud of your carpentry work, Zoel."

I hadn't thought of canoe building as carpentry work, but he might be right. I definitely had enjoyed building the canoes and the wigwams and wondered if there were other things I could build. Then I thought about the baby, so I approached Anna with my idea. "Anna, I would like to build something for the baby to sleep in."

She was delighted. "Oh, Zoel, that would be wonderful!"

After she described what she would need, I headed off to see the canoe builder. He told me what to do and where to find the materials I would need. He also showed me two types of baby cradles that were in his son's wigwam. One was larger than the other, but they both had woven wicker tied to an ash frame. He showed me how to shape the legs so the cradle wouldn't fall over—definitely an important bit of information.

I began my search for the supplies. A few days later, the canoe builder examined my work and made a few noteworthy suggestions. He was an expert craftsman; I liked working with experts. Two days later, the cradle was finished. When I gave it to Anna, she glowed with pleasure, thanked me, and gave me a big, big hug.

Again, with Henry's pen and paper, I wrote down how to properly build a cradle. Henry even gave me a leather folder to keep my notes in. "Looks like the start of a new book," he said. I told him about Josh's note-taking on beaver locations. He was impressed.

The next day, Josh and Yancy arrived. It was great to see them lumber into the village. They were carrying large, heavy packs of supplies. "You're bigger and taller," Yancy said to me as I helped him take off his pack. We exchanged manly hugs and handshakes. I had really missed them. Because so many of the others were also glad to see them, we ate supper outside; everyone brought food and drinks to share. The villagers were not only anxious to see what new items Josh and Yancy had to trade, but they were also anxious to find out what was new in Quebec City. It was a fun evening and just plain great to see our "family" back together again.

CHAPTER 2

Competition

Anna was comfortable with two of the midwives and wanted them both there when it was her time, and in her strong but subtle way, she let Henry know. I was delighted she wasn't going to travel until the baby was born. I was concerned about their health. I knew it was the loss of my folks that made me sensitive to unnecessary risk, but it was also the prudent thing to do.

The midwives said late summer was the earliest time Anna and the baby would be strong enough to travel, so Henry, Josh, Yancy, and I made our plans around that time frame. Henry believed he needed to travel down the Connecticut River and then east to visit other Indian villages. He had listened carefully to those who had traveled that area, and he felt in his heart he'd been called to set up a mission to care for sick and abandoned Indians somewhere near a huge lake and south of the mountains covered with snow most of the year. It was like a premonition, he said, and he couldn't get it out of his mind. However, he knew its timing was the Lord's.

He didn't want to place Anna and the baby at risk, so he was content with not leaving until late summer. I didn't care as long as the family stayed together.

Many of the warriors and braves were already hunting or trapping. "Seventy-five percent of the furs we'll deliver to Quebec City this summer will come from the villagers," Josh said, "and 25 percent will come from our small team."

He, Yancy, and I traveled to both of the areas we had trapped in the previous fall. We were successful in bringing home enough beaver to supplement the furs we had picked up from trading with our Abenaki hosts. We also provided a significant amount of smoked venison and turkey, as well as a moose, which helped feed the villagers during our stay.

Josh and Yancy were getting ready to deliver the load of furs to Quebec City. They had no trouble lining up warriors to make the trip with them. Those who had traveled with us on the previous trip had first dibs. Others were added as the inventory of furs grew. Henry saw no need to make the trip. He wanted to stay and continue on with teaching his French classes and weekly worship services. He was also involved in helping sick villagers; therefore, he was needed more where he was than with us delivering furs and picking up more trade goods. He knew I wanted to go, but he was concerned about my physical condition. However, Anna and my friend Sooleawa (silver) convinced him I was healthy enough to make the trip.

*   *   *

Since receiving my grandfather's letter from France, I felt the Lord was telling me to write back to encourage him. Henry sent his communications through Fathers Neel and Donne at the church in Quebec City and encouraged me to do the same. He said there was no organization as reliable as the church for communications and financial transactions. And, he said, although I should always keep them close, I shouldn't let them run my life. *Interesting,* I thought. I wrote back to my grandfather thanking him for his letter, for his well wishes, and for his offer to take me in when and if I traveled back to France.

Although I had enjoyed horses when I was younger, I didn't have any idea how to care for them. Nevertheless, I believed horses would materially enhance our ability to grow the trapping and trading business. I was pleased when both Josh and Henry agreed with me. Their agreement led me to ask my grandfather, in my letter, to help us by finding and shipping some horses to Quebec City. I told him we had earned sufficient profits in our trading and trapping business and believed it was appropriate to make an investment in at least one stallion and two mares, plus the cost of their shipping as estimated by Henry. I introduced Josh in my letter and shared about his experience with horses and his commitment to help me care for them.

I also wrote that horses had been shipped from France on two prior occasions. The second shipment had flourished and was doing well in Quebec City and in another trading post farther west on the St. Lawrence River, according to Josh's research. I told him many people wanted to get into the fur-trading business; and for us to be competitive, I felt we needed horses to carry trade goods and furs over longer distances.

Henry read the letter and told me the best way to get

action was to have Father Neel or Father Donne transfer the money from my account through the church and have it delivered to my grandfather along with my letter. Henry said, "If your grandfather doesn't think it's a good investment, the money will be returned."

Planning for the next step in our partnership was done. It was becoming obvious to me that Henry would be focusing more on investing his profits in the mission, and that I would be investing mine in growing the business. Josh and Yancy volunteered to invest some of their profits in buying and bringing the horses to Quebec City. My primary role, I suggested to them though, was investing in trade goods and ways of expanding the business and theirs was still in securing our safety and running the day-to-day business. I also reminded them I was still a teenager. They just laughed at that.

*   *   *

Anna had a baby girl right on time. They named her Nadie (wise) May Priest. She was healthy and needed space to build her lung strength. Henry and Anna wanted me to stay in the wigwam with them, but I wasn't really comfortable with the baby's crying during the night. They said they understood.

I thought about moving in with my friends Etu (sun) and Ezhno (solitary) because they had invited me to when I was recovering from the snakebite. But they were sweet on two village girls who had proven to be great cooks in a cooking contest they had judged. They had met with the girls' parents and plans were underway to deliver the gifts needed to accommodate both weddings. My time living with them would be short lived, so I decided against it.

Josh and Yancy said they had more room than they needed, so I moved in with them the next day. Immediately, I suggested the three of us build a wigwam closer to the creek. It would be a gift to the village. They said they would help some but trapping was their priority. I understood.

I wanted to build the wigwam while there were experienced people around to make sure I did it right. It was mainly my project while Josh and Yancy were off hunting and trapping. Like most other projects in the village, once it was started everyone pitched in. In a short time, it was finished. I asked Henry to make it a gift to the chief; he was delighted to do so. He complimented me by saying, "Zoel, you have been gifted with a builder's talent."

CHAPTER 3

A New World

Ten warriors were loaded and ready to travel. This time they knew exactly what they wanted to buy in Quebec City with the money they would earn toting the furs to the city and the trading goods back to the village. Their wives had made their desires known; the warriors were discussing it among themselves. Thanks to Henry and Anna, some of them spoke French fairly well. I thought it should prove to be an interesting trip.

Josh, Yancy, and I were packed and almost ready to head out. Henry wanted us to search out any new medicines in Quebec City that people had brought from France and made available for sale. He also wanted us to be sure to spend time with Father Neel and Father Donne and to invest in them as friends. I knew where he was coming from and told him not to worry. We would spend time with them and treat them well.

Henry was a relationship person and believed relationships had to be nurtured. He was also an independent thinker and could never be told what to preach and what not to preach.

Balancing his friendships with those he loved and respected in the church and, at the same time, maintaining his belief standards wasn't easy. But he was committed, and I wanted to help at every opportunity. I knew what he wanted us to do, which was to focus on Father Neel, Father Donne, and their needs. We told him we would do it.

We said our good-byes and were finally off. Having been sick most of the winter and now recovered, I needed a three-hundred-mile trip to get the kinks out of my body and mind. The snakebite had given me lots of time to study with Henry and to think through who I am and who I am not. I decided I was not Henry. I would have loved to have had his language ability and memory, but I didn't. I needed to learn to live within my own capabilities and interests.

With all that now behind me, I wanted to learn more about what I could do to help grow our trapping and fur-trading business. I would do my best to accomplish Henry's objectives on this trip. I would also keep my eyes open and try to learn more about our competition and what they may be doing better than we were.

* * *

The weather was perfect for our trip, and the demise of the renegade Indians made the trip much less stressful. My buddies Etu and Ezhno could have made the trip with us; but with their pending marriages, they felt they couldn't leave. I was sure they would be married by the time we got back to the village. I decided we had to do what we had to do. I was learning.

The long summer days provided lots of time to travel; and since no one got sick, we reached the river in twelve days flat. We saw a few trappers and two bands of Indians, but we weren't close enough to exchange words. There were more boats to take us across the St. Lawrence River to Quebec City now, and the competition had driven the prices down. Both Fathers Neel and Donne were glad to see us and offered their accommodations and facilities. Because it was summer, they were caring for only a few, they said.

The church had added a new section to the mini hospital, which enabled them to take care of more of the sick. The nuns now lived across the street and helped with the sick and those in need. The expansion was a separate building, but it was connected to the side of the church where they had made a new doorway. We settled down in the older part where we had stayed before.

The priests went with us to the trading post to complete all our financial transactions as they had done on the previous trip. After watching everything they did, I decided I'd handle the finances myself next time. Even though the trip was only half over, the warriors were delighted with their full payments.

Privately, both priests were pleased with Henry's and my 10 percent tithes. They asked me if I realized how unique our giving was in the community. I asked them to make sure it was kept private. I told them Henry would say we were just doing what the Bible instructed us to do—and he would be right. They agreed and asked me to thank him again. I assured them I would. As we were leaving the building, Josh and Yancy said they had tithed for the first time in their lives, and it felt good. I complimented them and hoped it was the work of the Holy Spirit.

Later at the church, I shared with the priests the plan Josh and I had to bring horses from France. Both priests agreed it was an excellent idea. They knew farmers with horses and suggested we visit them and learn all we could. They also agreed to help us find supplies of the new medicines for Henry. They said they would be more than happy to handle our mail and financial transactions with my grandfather. When they had handled Henry's and my grandfather's letters in the past, they had dealt with a church in the community in France where my grandfather lived so everything would be kept confidential.

The warriors had a great visit to the city, and those who knew French helped those who didn't. Josh, Yancy, and I visited two farms outside the city where the corn was already up to our hips. The farms were large compared to French farms. There were no stone barns or buildings yet, but there were stone walls. The farmers showed us their horses; it was just like being back in France. The horses were sturdy and strong, but they weren't huge. They could pull wagons, logs, and farm equipment, and they were more than strong enough to carry furs and trade goods as well as men the size of Josh and Yancy—which wasn't a light task. I think this was the first time Yancy had been this close to a horse, although he said he had seen some when he and Josh wintered in the city.

After I took notes of everything we learned, we all headed back to the church. It wasn't necessary for me to buy Henry or Anna a gift, but I did need to buy gifts for the baby and

Sooleawa. Baby clothes were scarce. Yancy knew everyone and directed me to a small home not far from the dressmaker's home we had visited on our previous trip. I bought Nadie two outfits she could grow into. I also found some delicate jewelry I was sure Sooleawa would like.

Josh, Yancy, and I talked with many of the tradesmen and workers in the trading post and quizzed them on any trapping innovations. No one so far was using horses, it appeared, but we did learn there were more trading posts farther down the St. Lawrence, and their production was picking up as production in the Quebec City area was leveling off. There were now multiple companies involved in setting up trading posts. Some were even buying furs at the shipping docks, so the price of beaver was going up. We were encouraged by that news. We knew Henry would also be encouraged.

With our tasks completed, I asked Fathers Neel and Donne—privately—if they needed anything special. "No," Father Neel responded, "just your safe return, Zoel." I thought that was nice. I handed him a gold piece, which I had previously removed from its hiding place in the lining of my coat in my backpack. I asked that they invest it wisely and thanked them again for their hospitality. I also told them I felt the gold was the Lord's money, and I was just holding it until He touched my heart and told me whom to give it to.

*   *   *

The trip back to the village was hard work for all of us. Many of the items we were carrying were heavy, including metal axes, metal pots and tripods, medicines and liquids for Henry, new seeds for different kinds of squashes, corn, and beans, and lots of clothes. Each warrior also carried the items he had bought for his family. We made many stops and didn't travel as far each day. Fortunately, the weather held up, and we didn't run into any renegade Indians or robbers.

Yancy did his scouting job as well as he always did. And we were careful to keep an eye out so we wouldn't be surprised by anyone. We met two families traveling together. They were very tired and hoped to reach the city within two days. We assured them they should be able to do that. I spent my time at the back of the team guarding the rear with my musket. I have to admit, it was loaded all the time. I was ready and willing to use it. I had suggested my new role to Josh and Yancy before we left Quebec City; they agreed it was a good idea. Knowing that no one was supposed to be behind me was unnerving at times. I would hear strange sounds and check them out and then hurry to catch up to the family again.

It was wonderful to finally arrive at the village after our long trip. Everyone was excited about what some called our "shopping trip" to Quebec City. Before we cleaned up for the welcome home celebration, we unpacked and stored all the trade goods in the storage wigwams. It was good to be home and not have to think about getting up in the morning to walk another ten or fifteen miles.

Henry, Anna, and my little sister, Nadie, were doing just fine. Sooleawa was as sweet as ever. The celebration was lots of fun for everyone. Anna loved the baby gifts, as did Henry. Sooleawa asked me to put her new jewelry on her; then she ran to Henry's wigwam to look in the small looking glass to see how it looked on her. She was back in a moment and thanked me with a hug and a big smile. It was great to see her happy. The dinner and dancing were fun; and the high, bright moon overhead made for a perfect evening.

I went to bed thinking about how much tougher it was going to be making the trips back and forth to Quebec City as we moved farther south down the valley of the Connecticut River—that is, unless we had horses.

Yancy and Josh were chatting about some pretty girls they had met at the celebration. That surprised me. Maybe Etu's and Ezhno's happy marriages and beautiful wives had triggered their interests. Who knows? But they were both enamored enough to talk me to sleep.

The beginning of a coat.
Courtesy of Jack Mann

CHAPTER 4

Business and Adventure

Late one evening as we were sitting by the fire, Henry said he needed to spread his wings. I asked him what he had on his mind. He suggested a trip down the Connecticut River to explore new territory. He always had things worked out in advance, so I asked, "What can I do to help?"

"Organize a small party to take us down the river in the canoes as far as the next village so we can meet some new people."

He was predictable. Before winter trapped us in, he wanted to box the next stage of our trip by scouting the river and, at the same time, searching for potential new trading customers and friends. "We have time to make another trip to Quebec City before winter if we focus on trading and trapping," I said.

He looked me in the eyes and said, "I want to do both, Zoel."

"May I think about it overnight and get back to you in the morning?"

"Yes, certainly you can. I'm learning you have unique planning skills, and I sincerely value your suggestions."

He sounded as though he really meant it. We talked about other things, including my favorite subject—horses—and his favorite subject—new ways to heal the sick.

For some reason, I do my best thinking when I go to sleep. I wake up with it all figured out—or close to it. I went to bed and was asleep in seconds. Before the sun came up, I had thought through my suggestions. I wrote them down and waited for Henry to come by. When he did, we headed to the creek. I noticed he had his line and a couple of worms ready to put on his bone fishhook. He asked me if I'd had a good night's sleep. He said he had because Nadie was now sleeping through the night; the wigwam was at peace again. As he weaved the worm onto the end of his fishhook, he asked, "Any new thoughts?"

"Yes, I have a few. We have two muskets, and they are both very intimidating. One musket should be with you and one with the team that travels to Quebec City.

"Josh knows the Connecticut River, and he is the best resource if trouble starts in a new village. In my opinion, he is equal to a minimum of ten-fighting Indians. Yancy is excellent at scouting and knows more people in and near Quebec City than Josh does. If there is a problem anywhere between here and Quebec City, he has resources there that Josh doesn't have. Therefore, I think you should travel with Josh down the Connecticut River, and I should travel with Yancy and handle the Quebec trip."

He sat there and tugged a little at his fishing line before saying, "I like it, Zoel. You have done well. Which warriors should I take with me, and which warriors should you take with you?"

"The Abenaki chief would be complimented if you took with you his two new council members as his representatives. Etu and Ezhno are terrific fighters and good company. I suggest you ask them to choose the warriors they would like to invite and then pay each one of them well."

"Again, I'm impressed," Henry said. "You have learned a lot about the men you have traveled with. Which ones will you and Yancy take with you?"

"I need to talk with Yancy first, but I hope he is comfortable with the group we took last time because they were excellent. Nevertheless, I want to share the selection process with him."

He nodded his head in agreement as he pulled on the fishing line again. I knew in my heart he wanted me to travel with him, but I wanted him to have the best protection available in unfamiliar territory. That protection was Josh and his musket, and we both knew it.

Henry called a partnership meeting and reviewed our plans for the fall. Josh and Yancy were pleased. Anna was not. She contained her disappointment—as a classy lady does—but I could see it in her face. She was very comfortable in her wigwam, with her new friends, and with her role as assistant teacher. With Henry traveling, she would take on more teaching responsibilities. And although she was good at it, she knew Henry would be missed by many in the village. Henry met with the chief to share our intentions. After their meeting, he told us we had the chief's blessing.

About a week later, a large party of Abenaki Indians from

a village across the Connecticut River visited our village and asked the chief for permission to trade with his guests. We were all impressed with their beaver and fox skins. They cleaned out most of our remaining trade goods.

Etu and Ezhno knew the visiting chief and many of his warriors because they had fought the renegade Indians together. Henry encouraged the chief to provide our guests with food and lodging for the night, which he did. Now with all the furs we needed and our trading inventory about gone, it was time to pack and head out for Quebec City again.

Yancy was pleased he was asked to choose the warriors who were to travel to Quebec City with us. He selected the same ones who had made the previous trip. By doing so, they each knew they had earned his respect. Traveling three hundred miles with heavy loads on our backs would be challenging for all of us, but now they could buy items for their families that had been unimaginable just a year before. Within a few days, we were about ready to go.

I asked Yancy what he thought about asking the villagers what they wanted us to shop for in Quebec City. He thought it was a good idea and told the ten warriors to spread it around. The next morning, I found myself sitting in front of our wigwam penning a special-order list. It was fun writing down everyone's name and what he would provide as furs for the items he wanted. I wasn't just taking orders. I was negotiating each trade and haggling back and forth—with a lot of laughter.

I finally finished the shopping list; and as a team, we finished packing furs and beaver vitals. We said our good-byes and then wished Josh and Henry a safe trip. Henry had some mail and notes he wanted me to deliver to the priests, as well as specific things he wanted me to buy for him. Sooleawa had made me some buckskin gloves and a buckskin hat, both lined with fur. They were beautiful and practical. I thanked her and complimented her on her work and asked her what she needed from Quebec City. She smiled and said, "Just your safe return." She thought I would blush or laugh. Instead, I surprised her and gave her a hug and whispered in her ear, "I'll do my best."

Yancy took the point again and scouted ahead. I knew the trail now as well as anyone, so I took the lead. I enjoyed planning the trip. As each day passed, I liked the point position more.

CHAPTER 5

Lawless Country

We were becoming old hands at finding our way to Quebec City. Everyone on the team had been there before and was looking forward to unloading his backpack at the trading outpost. The packs of furs were more bulky than heavy, but no one complained. Yancy didn't scout as far ahead as he normally did when Josh was along, I noticed. I figured he was concerned about me in my new role, which was okay with me.

We didn't usually follow each other directly. Josh had taught us it would be easy for someone to pick us off if we did so. Therefore, we spread out but kept each other in sight. We followed the same rules we had when Henry and Josh were with us. We saw no reason to change them. I kept my musket loaded and ready; everyone else kept bows and arrows ready.

The weather was warm and humid, but none of us were out of shape. We ate light and kept our eyes open. The forest was alive with the sights and sounds of birds as well as animals.

The ponds were loaded with toads and frogs and fish. When I stood at the water's edge for a few minutes, the activity I saw was surprising. It was both a hunter's and a fisherman's paradise. Hawks and eagles of all kinds flew overhead and fought each other over food. In the late mornings, the turkeys came out of the trees and made gobbling, clucking, and yelping sounds.

I always enjoyed the deer. The bucks snorted and made various noises when they were interrupted or surprised. The lynx and bobcats took long looks at us and then continued doing whatever they were doing. The young bobcats were my favorite, especially the females. When they walked, they sauntered.

Our communications on the trip had changed from speaking Nipmuck to speaking Abenaki-Penobscot to accommodate our warriors. They talked very little on the trail. However, once we stopped for the night, it was chatter time. Everyone pitched in and the routines became automatic. The summer days were long, and we tried not to waste precious time. The closer we got to the New France area, the more on guard we were for robbers and renegade warriors. With anyone being able to sell furs to owners of ships at the docks, we had been warned during our previous visit to keep our eyes open for small bands of Indians led by Frenchmen.

We took turns at night being on guard duty and switched off frequently to prevent anyone from going to sleep. While preparing evening meals, at least two warriors were hiding and watching for intruders. Yancy predicted we would be attacked soon because the price of beaver was going up as its availability was diminishing in New France.

I was sitting high in a maple tree and overlooking the campsite and the long valley toward the St. Lawrence River. We were one or two days away from the river and vigilant for robbers. I spotted two individuals headed up the valley toward us. I couldn't tell if there were more. I immediately climbed down out of the tree, ran to the campsite, and called everyone together. The fire was hot and supper was just about ready.

Yancy ran to bring in the other guard who was on the other side of the campsite. They were back in just a few minutes. I reported what I had seen. Yancy outlined what we had to do. We quickly hid our packs under branches cut from bushes and collected our weapons. Then we spread out and climbed the trees facing the direction from which Yancy thought they would approach the campsite. He said we needed to wait until they were in the camp in full view and then my musket was the signal to shoot to kill.

Because one of the men looked like a French trapper, Yancy thought they may be part of a small band of robbers. We wouldn't know until they arrived, so it was critical we made every shot count. He said, "Stay hidden until you hear the musket; then fire your arrows, drop to the ground, and attack with your tomahawks and knives. Remember, we were told during our last visit that 'the robbers leave no survivors.' "

We waited. Yancy was in the next tree. The fire was still cooking the venison; it smelled sweet. They were a small group of seven Indians and two Frenchmen. The Frenchmen had muskets and the robbers' weapons were loaded and pointed at the campfire. A Frenchman with a musket was in the lead; the others were walking almost parallel to him. Yancy pointed to the lead man with the musket, which indicated to me he was my target. I waited and couldn't believe how shaky I became. It was like having buck fever.

They were walking slowly and looking everywhere for us as they approached our trees. I had my target in sight and was ready to fire. I looked over at Yancy; he mouthed the word *now*. I aimed at the Frenchman's upper body and fired. I saw him go down. I immediately reloaded and looked for the other Frenchman. Unable to find him, I dropped from the tree. The arrows were flying from the trees as I searched for him. It was bedlam.

Yancy got to him first with his tomahawk. He just rolled over on the ground. We looked for others. Our Abenaki warriors had done their jobs well. None of the attempted robbers lived past the engagement. All the bodies were collected and carried closer to the fire pit. We collected their weapons and anything of value they had carried. We searched the direction they had come from and found some backpacks of furs and travel items and brought them to the center of the campsite. We all looked at Yancy for instruction. He said we had done an excellent job. Now it was time to honor the dead and then bury them and cover them with stones to protect their bodies from the animals.

I asked Yancy to keep the muskets as his own and suggested the others divide up any of the items they wanted and then bury everything else with the bodies. They all agreed. Just before dark, we were done and cleaned up. We collected our packs of furs and personal items, added wood to the fires, and restarted our preparations for supper. There had been very little talking since the firefight; we were all very tired. Supper was light but satisfying. I wasn't ready to sleep, so I suggested Yancy and I take the first watch and the rest catch some sleep.

I had the chills as I sat on a small hill above the camp. I hoped they would go away soon. It wasn't the night air that caused them. It was the realization I had just helped kill nine people. I prayed the Lord would draw the family and me close tonight and help us get past the horror of what had transpired. After a couple of hours had passed, I walked back to camp and noticed Yancy was having something to eat again. As I walked up to him, he asked, "Are you all right?"

"I have been better."

"If you stay in the trading and trapping business, Zoel, this will not be the last time this happens, and you will never get used to it."

"I notice you don't have the muskets with you, Yancy."

"I felt certain that if I kept them someone would eventually recognize them, and I'd be in big trouble. So I buried both with their owners. They will never be seen again."

"Good idea. I didn't think of it that way."

"We can't continue to survive if you don't have a musket, Yancy. Will you let me buy you a custom-made one when we reach the city?"

"That will work as long as there is a record you purchased it for me and many others in the city also know it.

"Then let's do it."

The morning came too soon for me. I took a look at the graves. They were off the trail and covered with stones, but not with markers. The entire area was actually pretty with wild flowers growing not far away and with many trees shading the graveyard. I was certain the bushes would grow and cover the graves in less than a season. I felt bad that what happened had to happen, but this was lawless country. We had to protect ourselves. We headed out a little later—quieter than usual—but we picked up the pace knowing we only had one more night in the woods.

CHAPTER 6

From Bad to Good

The river was within our grasp, but I didn't feel the same as I had in the past when we were nearly home. I had felt safer in the Abenaki village than I now did in New France. *Amazing!* It was interesting how having been attacked by renegades and robbers had changed my perspective of a sanctuary so quickly.

This was the first time I was able to complete our business and financial transactions without the help of Fathers Neel or Donne. As soon as we finished our business at the trading post, we headed to the church to unpack, clean up, and collect ourselves. We met Father Neel and Father Donne. As usual, they welcomed us with open arms. The church was always a sanctuary—but of a different sort. I felt the Lord's presence in this church and the peace that flowed from the Holy Spirit.

The warriors all knew what they wanted to shop for and headed to the trapper's store. We agreed to meet back at the church for supper. Yancy and I searched out the musket maker. At first, I didn't tell him the musket was for Yancy, but it didn't take long for him to figure it out. Yancy knew what he wanted and outlined his desires to the craftsman in detail. He also wanted a soft leather cover that could be quickly and easily removed.

When the craftsman looked up at me, I smiled and said, "This weapon is a gift for my partner for protecting my life as well as that of many others in our family over the past year."

The craftsman replied, "You are blessed to have such a friend. I need three days to make your gift. When I finish it, I'll deliver it to the church."

"That will be perfect." I signed a draft on my account at the trading post for the full amount. The musket maker was pleased.

Yancy suggested we head down to the river and check out the fur-trading activity. The ships seemed to be larger than the one I had traveled in not so long ago. There was absolutely no activity on the dock. We walked up to a ship and looked around. One of the ship's employees asked us if there was something he could do for us. I asked, "What are you paying for beaver furs and vitals?"

He gave me a quote. It was higher than what we had received from the trading post. That surprised me. "Are you paying in gold and silver?"

"Always," he replied.

That's interesting, I thought. We thanked him and moved on.

We found a place in the shade to relax, but we kept our eyes on the dock. After two hours of no activity, I suggested we move on. Yancy pointed down the street to a group headed our way. One Frenchman and three Indians were loaded with pelts. They looked around as they entered the dock. The Frenchman was almost as big as Josh and carried a musket. Yancy said he had seen him before, and he wasn't a trapper or a trader. While we watched the entire transaction, I wondered why the government agents allowed the sale of furs to ship owners. It only appeared to motivate thieves to steal furs and then to sell them.

On our way back to the church, we stopped at the trapper's store and ordered all the items on Henry's and Josh's lists as well as the items we needed. When we got back to the church, I asked Father Neel why he thought the agents would allow the ship owners to traffic in stolen goods. He answered, "The government collects a percent of the purchase price as a fee no matter which company buys it. The more transactions that take place, the more money the government collects. Keep in mind, the ships are owned by competitive trading companies." He went on to say, "Now on a different subject, I have some mail for you and Henry."

A letter had arrived from my grandfather. In it he expressed his excitement about our success in the fur-trading business and said he had selected the horses for shipment in the spring. He said he wanted to come with them, but his health wasn't good enough to make the trip. He noted he had returned the money and wanted to pay for the horses and the shipment and to become my silent partner. I was more excited about him becoming my silent partner than I was about the money. He also mentioned he was not a Catholic and wanted to remind me that years ago King Louis XIII forbade anyone who was not a Roman Catholic to buy property in New France, so he had to keep that in mind.

It took a little while longer to buy the special items the Abenaki villagers wanted. We did eventually find everything because what they ordered were basic items we had already traded, but there was more of a variety than we usually purchased. I had to make sure I didn't miss anybody's order. I'm not sure how smart my special ordering had been when I considered I was going to have to label everything before we packed it for shipment. Yancy just laughed as we worked together to fill and pack the orders. He said, "You did a good thing and God will reward you," and then he laughed again. The ordered items only took up about half of our capacity, so we bought plenty of additional items to trade with other villages. We finally finished, and the warriors stopped by to help us haul it all back to the church.

Yancy and I took a few minutes with Fathers Neel and Donne and gave them our tithes as well as Henry's and Josh's. As usual, they thanked us graciously. I quietly met alone with them and shared the content of my grandfather's letter and asked them if what he had said about King Louis XIII was true. They nodded their heads yes. That didn't sit well with me.

Father Donne asked me for a favor. "Would you consider taking someone with you?"

"Perhaps, but tell me more."

"Well, we have many parishioners in our church who are poor. This particular family was both sick and poor. We tried to help them, but the parents died. They were not Catholic, the child is not Catholic, and no one will adopt him. He is a problem. We're feeding and caring for him, but he is a bit much for us. If you would take him with you, maybe he could be successful as a trapper and trader some day. He speaks some French, but he is English. He has no family, and no one else will help him, Zoel. Many people here hate the English."

My heart skipped a beat. This was me on the boat, and I was rescued by Henry. *How can I refuse to help him?* I asked myself. "Where is he?"

"He is staying with a family while you and your team are here; he will return to the church after you leave. His name is Peter Smith."

That stopped me cold. I excused myself and looked for Yancy. He was busy helping the warriors tighten their packs, but when he looked up and saw my serious, troubled look, he asked, "What's wrong, Zoel?"

"I need some advice, Yancy," He quickly stepped away from the others. Once out of their hearing range, I told him about Father Donne's request.

"Isn't your last name Smith?"

"Yes, it is, but I'm sure we aren't related. Even so, I feel I have no choice but to take him on as a brother. God has touched my heart, Yancy, and I need to help them and him. Please tell me what *you* think."

"Our God is a good God and loves the poor and wants us to raise them up as Henry has taught us. That's why Josh and I now tithe. We want to do what God wants us to do. How can we walk away from this boy? I promise no matter how many problems he has, you and I will be his brothers," he said, placing his hands assuredly on my shoulders. "I will help you."

I love this man, I said to myself, as I walked back to the church.

"Are there some legal papers we need to sign, Father Donne?" There were none. He left immediately to collect the boy and his things.

"He will need some things to travel," I told Father Neel.

"We have already prepared him for travel, Zoel. We know your heart and thank you."

I removed one piece of gold from my sewed hide-a-way. He smiled as he watched me remove it and then thanked me again.

Peter Smith looked healthy with his hair sticking out from under his cap. He asked if we were related. I told him the odds were good we were distant relatives, but only time would tell. He gave me an understanding look. I introduced him to Yancy and the warriors and told them he was a new family member and looked forward to traveling with us. They were all gracious and introduced themselves. *I can't wait to write to my grandfather again,* I thought.

The musket maker delivered Yancy's gift along with all the powder, flints, balls, straps, cover, and cleaning tools he needed. The warriors were excited and Fathers Neel and Donne were impressed. We thanked the gifted craftsman for his hard work. We were now ready to head to our Abenaki home. I looked across the room and hoped Peter Smith was ready.

CHAPTER 7

The Smith Brothers

Having someone younger with us on the trail added a new feeling of responsibility. During the first few days, Peter was quiet. But as he appeared to become comfortable with the routines, he opened up a little. He followed me closely and carried all his personal items in a backpack. He asked me a few questions about where we were going and how far away it was. I didn't think he was concerned about the distance because he had plenty of energy. In the evening of the third day, he asked if he could sleep near me. I told him that would be fine. "Are you cold at night?" I asked.

"No, I'm just uncomfortable sleeping alone."

I said my prayers before I went to sleep. When I opened my eyes, I noticed he was watching me. "Father Neel said your parents died sickly like mine," he said.

"Yes, that's true, Peter."

"How can you love and pray to a God who killed your parents?"

"My God didn't kill my parents. The sickness did, Peter.

My God found me a new dad to take care of me and to love me."

He went to sleep, and I lay awake thinking about how bitter he must feel about the loss of his parents. I was overwhelmed when my folks died as he also must have been, but I had Henry. During the night, he woke me up as he snuggled up against me. It made me uncomfortable for a few moments, and then I went back to sleep. In the morning, I asked him to help start the fire while I got some food ready to cook. He said he didn't know how to, so I showed him. I also asked him to collect more firewood and told him what to look for.

He learned quickly, and the warriors made him feel like he was part of our family. He showed no obvious fear of either people or the forests, and he seemed excited with every new animal and bird he saw. It was great to listen to him hum once in a while. It reminded me of having Etu walking behind me. I started humming Etu's song. Peter quickly picked it up; we hummed it together and laughed. It was the first time I heard him laugh.

Yancy was scouting again, and I was on point. Each day that passed, we felt more comfortable because we were farther away from Quebec City and the risk of robbers and renegades. I was sure most people in the city felt just the opposite, and I realized how much more like the Indian warriors I was becoming. The violent attempted robbery and killings were still in the back of my mind, but I wasn't going to let them steal my joy. As we traveled home, I prayed many times each day that the Lord would keep the devil away from me and not let him steal my joy.

We stopped at a familiar lake and decided to stay for a day

and relax, fish, and hunt for venison. Summer was passing. The water was cooler, but it was perfectly refreshing. Peter couldn't swim, so Yancy and I spent some time teaching him with a small dry branch. The branch helped him keep his head above water as he learned to kick his way through it. After a midday snack, we went back into the lake. This time he swam without the branch. It was fun watching him learn. He certainly wasn't afraid to try new things.

The days were comfortable, the evenings were cooling off, and we were all looking forward to uninterrupted travel the rest of the way home. We talked a lot about the attempted robbery. It was good to get it out of our systems. Many of the warriors had been part of the band that had killed the renegades. They said it was tough and took a long time to track down every member of the renegade band. But in the end, they had all been buried the same way we buried the attempted robbers—with their toes pointed up at the stars.

Although the past two days had been rainy ones, we kept going. Our packs were covered with deerskins, so nothing inside got wet. Peter had asked if we were going to stop, and when I had told him we weren't, he responded, "Good, I love the rain."

Only two days were left. We were getting excited. At every turn on the trip home, Peter had pleasantly surprised Yancy and me. The night before our arrival, Yancy stayed in camp. The three of us sat together at supper and talked. Yancy asked Peter how he felt about the trip. He said he loved it, especially the animals. We tried to prepare him for his new temporary home by telling him he would live in a wigwam with Yancy, me, and our friend Josh. He seemed comfortable with that.

When I asked if he had any questions, he said, "I hope your dad and mom will like me."

He broke my heart. I told him I was sure they would, but the look on his face told me he wasn't convinced.

*   *   *

We entered the village in late morning. It was busy. Everyone was back from the trip downriver; all had gone well. Henry and Anna fell in love with Peter Smith the moment they met him. Henry asked me if I minded if they invited him to live with them. I said I was delighted. Privately, Anna thanked me and said, "We would at least like for him to live with us until he recovers from the loss of his parents."

Josh was pleased I had given Yancy the musket. "You did the right thing. You'll never regret it."

We delivered all our special requested items and put the furs we received in trade away in inventory. Yancy and Josh suggested we travel to the Abenaki villages soon and trade what we had bought before winter arrived. I thought it was an excellent idea. "I missed you guys," Josh admitted. We admitted we had missed him, too, and meant it.

I asked Josh how Etu's and Ezhno's weddings went. He said everyone had a wonderful time, and the guys wanted me to know I was no longer invited to live with them. I laughed and decided it was too late to visit them that evening, but I would make it a point to visit them the next day. Josh said he wanted us to meet the young lady he had committed to marry. Yancy and I just looked at each other. We were speechless! "How about ... meeting her tomorrow?" I finally asked.

"Tomorrow it will be, Lord willing," Josh said. Yancy and I were too stunned to say anything more.

The next day, we were busy visiting our friends and bringing each other up to date on missed happenings. Everyone was well, including my baby sister, Nadie. She was growing and ready to travel, but it appeared there would be no travel until next spring. Anna was pleased she could stay in this village one more winter with her new friends. Josh's lady friend was healthy and strong and physically a good match for him. I could see them trapping, trading, and traveling back and forth together to Quebec City.

The crops had done well, Henry said, and most of the village was getting ready for winter. He asked me about the attempted robbery and how it had gone for me. I told him, "Killing robbers is not what I do best, but I learned if I had to do it, I could."

He said he was pleased with my gift to Yancy, especially the cover that kept it out of sight when it was appropriate. He asked if it was my idea. I told him it was Yancy's, which pleased him even more. He said, "You and Yancy are like brothers, Zoel."

"I think you're right, Henry. And he and Josh are coming much closer to the Lord, thanks to you and the Holy Spirit." He just smiled.

We talked about Peter Smith. Henry was excited and referred to him as the Lord's gift. "I hope you don't mind our interest in him."

"Of course I don't. Peter needs parents like you and Anna. And the more you get involved in his life, the happier I will be."

I shared everything Fathers Neel and Donne had shared with me, including the letter from my grandfather. Henry mentioned I would have to be in Quebec City in the spring to collect my horses without Josh if he got married. I agreed. "I'm sure Yancy and I will be taking another trip there with furs in the spring. We can pick up the horses then. We should be able to follow you when you relocate farther down the Connecticut River."

"Most likely, we'll wait for your return before we leave. It would be much more fun to travel together again, especially with two new muskets and three new horses."

CHAPTER 8

Sooleawa's Joy

Sooleawa was fully grown and ready for marriage, Anna told me privately while we sat and watched Nadie play. I wasn't surprised at Sooleawa's maturity because she appeared to have recovered fully from her terrible experience, and she had invested much of her time learning French and acquiring many new skills. "Anna, what's on your mind?" Please be candid with me for Sooleawa's sake."

"You come and go and then come and go again. You are not here much, and she is ready for a long-term relationship with you as her husband. She is strong enough to travel with you if you are going to travel, and she is ready to have your children if you are ready to settle down. What are your plans, Zoel?"

Anna was direct and concerned about her best friend's happiness. I had been aware of that since we first met. "What does Henry think about the two of us, Anna?"

She looked away. I knew the answer. Henry and Anna

didn't agree on the marriage. Henry would say I was too young.

"I will do everything I can to help Sooleawa. She was wonderful to me when I was sick, and she has been a very close friend. My only concern, Anna, is what is best for Sooleawa. I don't think I'm the best man for her—at least not yet. But I think you're right. She is ready for marriage, but I'm not. One day she told me I shouldn't worry about us being together. She said if God wanted us together, we would be if we both prayed about it and did what we felt He was leading us to do. I think she was right."

"Are you going to tell her you're not ready for marriage yet?"

"If that's what's best for Sooleawa, I will tell her tomorrow. Do you think she wants to know where my heart is now? Is she interested in someone else?"

"I think the answer is yes to both questions."

Nadie crawled up on my lap and got comfortable and started pulling on my shirt buttons. She looked a lot like Anna and had a wonderful disposition. Peter and Henry were visiting with the chief and his son and would be back soon. I had time to ask one more question. "In your opinion, Anna, what do *you* think is best for Sooleawa?"

"She should marry an Abenaki warrior and spend the rest of her life here with her new family and friends if you are not ready to settle down and spend the rest of your life in this village."

I thanked her and gave her and Nadie each a kiss on the cheek, said good night, and then headed back to my wigwam.

I knew I wasn't ready to spend the rest of my life in that village, although I had many friends there. I would miss Sooleawa's close friendship, but I didn't want to mislead her if she was ready for marriage. I figured I would do what was right in the morning. While I was still alone in the wigwam, I prayed about it and asked God to reconfirm my decision and then give me the appropriate words to say to Sooleawa. I then put some more wood on the fire, had a few bites of cornbread, and waited for Yancy and Josh. They would be back soon; then I would go to bed. I thought tomorrow might be a tough day.

Winter was on its way. I could feel it in the morning air. I added more wood to the fire and started to make breakfast. It didn't take long for the water to boil and for the vegetables and turkey meat to thicken the stew. I stirred it carefully with a steel ladle until it was ready. It tasted good. I didn't have any idea when Josh and Yancy got to bed because I had dropped off to sleep before they arrived.

"It smells good, Zoel," Josh said, as he rolled over and got out of bed.

"It's the dark meat from the turkey that makes it smell so sweet, I think."

"I hope my new wife is as good a cook as you are."

"I bet if she's not you wouldn't marry her. When's the big event to take place?"

"We're about ready ... maybe in a week or so. We had to get her parents comfortable with the fact she wouldn't be living in the village much longer. They appear to be accepting it now."

"I'm happy for you, Josh. You waited a long time to find the right woman."

"Yes, I did, and you need to do the same thing. Don't be in a hurry at your age. The right one will come along in time. I had to find the Lord before I found the right woman."

"I am now more than pleased, Josh. When did you give your heart to Jesus?" I asked excitingly.

"It was on our trip down the river a few weeks ago when your team was delivering the furs to Quebec City. As Henry was praying for you, I realized you were in God's hands, and I wanted to be there also. Amazing, isn't it?"

"It truly is, Josh. It's a miracle."

Yancy was up now and dishing himself out some breakfast. The Lord had answered two prayers before breakfast: He had called Josh to himself, and He had confirmed through Josh I had made the right decision about Sooleawa. It was already a very good day.

*   *   *

Later that morning, I went to Sooleawa's wigwam. She was sitting down next to the doorway sewing. She said hello and set her sewing aside as I offered my hand to help her up. We talked small talk for a few moments as we walked. I told her we were getting ready to visit some of the Abenaki villages on the other side of the river, and I wanted to talk with her before we left. She was silent. But as I started to talk about her and our relationship, she abruptly interrupted me.

"I have been asked to marry ... I should have told you sooner, Zoel, but I couldn't. I didn't want to hurt your feelings

48

because we have been such close friends. But you need to know I am going to say yes. We will be married in a few weeks."

"I'm ... I'm happy God has found you the right partner, Sooleawa, and I truly wish you the best."

Obviously relieved, she smiled and said, "Thank you, Zoel. That means a lot to me." Then we shared a friendly hug.

During the walk back to her wigwam, she described her happiness and how she and her future husband had met. She told me his first wife had been killed in the attack by the renegade warriors. He had a young son, and the two of them loved to fish together. She said Henry was teaching them French and about Jesus.

It had been a great day. A good friend had found her mate, and I was still free. I had also learned a meaningful lesson: it appeared to me that men don't pick women; women pick men. Marriage looked great from a distance, and I was delighted I had not been chosen. I really wasn't ready. In fact, I was a long way away from being ready.

CHAPTER 9

What We Don't See

Yancy and I were ready to make a few trips to some Abenaki villages situated on the other side of the river. We asked Etu and Ezhno if they were interested in earning some extra silver. They declined but suggested we offer the opportunity to some of the single warriors who had traveled with us to Quebec City.

That started Yancy thinking about not just some short trips to Abenaki villages but maybe a long trip that would include us wintering in Quebec City. He said, "We're still single and don't need to spend the winter in wigwams attending weddings. Instead, we can be making some money and sleeping in a warm house and eating excellent meals."

This was new territory for me, so I suggested we meet with Henry. Henry thought it was a good idea as long as we stayed with Fathers Neel and Donne in Quebec City and, with the chief's permission, took at least six braves with us. We didn't have a lot of time; but if we planned it right, we could trade the goods in inventory for furs and hopefully get them to Quebec

City before it snowed. I met with the chief, and Yancy chased down the single warriors who had previously made the trip. In two days, we had the chief's blessings, seven committed warriors, and the remaining trade goods and some furs we had recently traded for, packed. We were ready to go.

Josh said he wanted to join us, but Yancy and I didn't believe him. We had our normal early morning breakfast with Henry before we left. It was like a quiet celebration before the sun was fully up. We built a fire in an outside pit and cooked some thin venison strips, bean soup, and cornbread with honey. Josh and Henry did all the cooking. It sure tasted great. We packed some smoked meat, corn, and beans to eat on the trip, but we knew we would eat little. We wanted our stamina to build fast because we had at least two hundred miles to travel, including visiting the villages, before swinging northeast to Quebec City.

We headed north on the river and then inland. Each visit was productive, and the trade goods were appreciated. The furs were excellent; many were beaver pelts. We honored each chief with a special gift and were invited back. The exciting part of each visit was when they learned Yancy had a musket. Some warriors in the villages had heard about them but hadn't seen one.

We went back to the river with the bulk of our trade goods gone and our packs loaded with furs. We paddled back to the east side and stopped at a small village. After we gave the chief a gift and traded goods for furs, they invited us to not only to a venison feast but to stay overnight as well. The roasted venison was delicious, and the social time was refreshing.

They agreed to keep our canoes for us until spring. In turn, we gave them the remainder of our goods.

Yancy said we were going to run into some snow, so everybody checked his personal packs to be certain he had dry and warm clothing. Fully rested, the next morning we repacked the furs and began the long journey to Quebec City. Yancy didn't scout ahead on this part of the trip. He and I had agreed there was no need. Since we both had a musket, we would lead the team together yet stay enough yards apart so as not to become easy targets.

We didn't run into anyone on the trail. Yancy said it was too cold for most to travel. After two light snowstorms and a lot of cold nights, we were finally facing the St. Lawrence River. The memories of the robbers' attack and deaths were in the back of my mind, but I was emotionally over the experience. We all loaded onto two boats, crossed the river, and then headed to the church. Everyone stayed outside while I went in to find Father Donne. He was in his office.

The church facilities were overloaded with mostly sick Indians. Father Donne suggested we rent a fairly good-sized home belonging to one of the church members who had returned to France for the winter. It had plenty of room, he said, for all of us. The owners had asked the priests to help them find someone trustworthy to rent it. He asked us to wait until Father Neel was free. Then they would help us get settled in the home.

I felt experienced enough to handle the financial matters, so I told him we would be back later to collect the keys and get directions to the home we would be renting. He was pleased with that and invited us to stay for supper. I politely declined his invitation by saying, "Considering the number of sick you are caring for, it might be better for our Abenaki friends if we stayed away from the church for now." He agreed.

I enjoyed managing the financial transactions knowing that Yancy and Josh had come to respect my skills in that area. Yancy, now fluent in French, witnessed every transaction, including the payment in full to each of the warriors and the crediting to each of our partnership accounts of an equal share after expenses. Certificates were also provided for each of us. We collected the gold and silver we needed for tithing and spending. Then we headed back to the church to collect the house keys and directions.

On the way back, I mentioned to the family as a group that there was some sickness around and that they might want to be careful and boil all eating utensils before and after using them. I said I knew I was going to. And, I added, we shouldn't eat any uncooked foods, and we should wash and then boil our clothes. Yancy, having spent many winters in Quebec City, told us the rules of survival were mandatory for Indians specifically and included staying away from crowds, not touching strangers, and making sure you didn't eat anything that hadn't been cooked or washed in vinegar.

After we arrived at the church, I told Father Neel I would personally make sure we left the rental as clean, if not cleaner, than we found it on our arrival. He said he wasn't worried about that. Yancy and I gave him the partnership's 10 percent tithe. He thanked us and said it had come just in time to help them care for the growing number of sick Indians in the mission. I invited him and Father Donne to supper the following evening, which would give us time to get set up and rested. He appreciated and accepted the invitation.

The house was just outside of town on the same road we had previously taken to visit the two farms with horses. It was a large building with lots of room and well built for cold winters with its multiple fireplaces. It wasn't the kind of house a lady would like. It was more of a working house for men. Yancy worked with the warriors getting them settled into their quarters. I set about organizing our things in the kitchen. There was a separate section for a family with its own small kitchen, but it didn't look as if it had been used much.

I started a fire in the kitchen and then moved on and started ones in two other fireplaces. There was plenty of kindling to start the fires and lots of hardwood stacked outside for the winter. The house warmed up slowly as we all settled in and began to prepare supper. Tired, we looked forward to getting to bed early. It had been a profitable and safe trip so far; we had a lot to be thankful for.

The next morning, we scouted the town—avoiding any busy places—and ended up down on the docks. It was interesting to see everybody trying to get his last shipment out before the winter ice set in. We saw two ships docked in fairly low water. It appeared they were about loaded and ready to head for France. That reminded me to give Fathers Neel and Donne our mail for France when they came to supper. It was midmorning, and the wind was blowing. It was chilly by the docks, so we all decided to head back to the house.

We each had some repair work to do on our clothes, weapons, or packs, and what we brought with us had to be washed and boiled. We began the process. Yancy and

I encouraged the warriors to make themselves comfortable while we shopped for essential items for our stay. We were all looking forward to having supper with our friends and hearing the local news. I was interested in learning if they had heard anything more from my grandfather.

*   *   *

As Yancy and I walked to the trapper's store, I asked him, "What are you doing with the money you are making from the business?"

"Do you really want to know?"

"Yes. If you are investing it, I really want to know."

He laughed and told me to follow him. He walked me to an older part of town not far from the river. The streets were narrow and the houses were more like shacks. He stopped at one of the better-looking places and knocked on the front door. A female voice said, "Come in."

Yancy opened the door. I followed him in. It was Chepi (fairy), the Indian lady we had met at the dress shop during a previous visit. She greeted Yancy with a big hug and welcomed him back. There was a lot more room in the house than there appeared to be from the street. Two mature adults were sitting at a table, and at least half a dozen young girls were playing in the next room. The place smelled as homes do when there is a terrific cook in the kitchen.

The lady shook my hand as Yancy introduced me as his partner and giver of the musket. I told her I remembered her from the store, and my lady friend loved the clothes I had bought there.

Yancy said everyone in the home was extended family. "Are you serious?" I asked.

"Well, in a way they are. Chepi, a widow, shares the house with a mutual lady friend of ours. The two senior adults are Chepi's father-in-law and mother-in-law. The girls are survivors of a sickness that killed their parents. Chepi works for the local dressmaker and, with the help of our friend, cares for her in-laws and the girls."

"God bless you, Yancy. You continue to amaze me. Do you own the house?"

"No, you have to be a Catholic to buy property in New France, so we just rent it. We also rent another place nearby. Would you like to see it?"

Yancy told Chepi he would be back the next day. We said our good-byes and headed out and over two streets.

On the river side of the street was a large barn-shaped building with a small door facing the street. Yancy opened it, and we walked down a short hallway that had two windows. At the end of the hallway was another door. He knocked on this one. A male voice hollered, "Come in."

We stepped inside a huge workshop. Two boats sitting on blocks looked to be under repair. There was a large fireplace in one corner of the workshop. Sitting and eating at a table in front of the fireplace were three teenage Indian braves and two older men. They all got up quickly, came over, and greeted Yancy.

Again, I was introduced as his partner and giver of the new musket. As we walked around and looked at the boats, Yancy encouraged them to get back to eating their food while it was hot. Comfortable living quarters were on the other side of the warehouse. The bedrooms were large and had at least three beds in each with rows of clothes hanging on wall racks. Each room had a fireplace and a window with shutters. On the back of the building, which faced the river, were large barn doors. At a second look, I noticed wooden runners under the boats and under the doors.

"I can't believe this, Yancy. Is this all yours?"

"No. Three of us—including Josh—own it."

He opened one of the rear barn doors. The land and the wooden rails sloped to the river. "The river is down about twenty feet," he said, "but it comes up to about five feet from the barn footing in the spring. Josh and I invested in the repair shop to help a French couple he had known when he lived in France. At the suggestion of a government agent, the couple decided to move to New France to start a boat repair business." He also told me, "The two men sitting at the table are excellent tradesmen from France, and the three Indian boys' parents had died from sicknesses a year ago."

"I appreciate your sharing this with me, Yancy. You appear to have invested well."

"We had a good year, and the boys are learning quickly. There's plenty of work for them. After Josh gets married, I'm sure he'll live here part of the time and help his friends, but I don't see him living here all the time. He loves trapping too much."

We said good-bye to everyone and headed back to accomplish our task, which was to stock the house with all the essentials for at least a week. While we were shopping, I couldn't unwind my thoughts. From day one, I knew Yancy was different. He didn't even look like an Indian warrior when I first met him. There was no feather in his hair, and he didn't paint his face. In reflection, I should have expected more. I knew he had depth and a good heart. What I didn't know was how generous he was to those who had nothing. He overwhelmed me today with his giving and caring spirit for people in need. Yancy was special. And I was thankful God had allowed me to be his friend and partner.

Warm and dry.
Courtesy of Jack Mann

CHAPTER 10

The Real World

We had made some progress at cleaning our equipment and clothes, but we had to interrupt the process to prepare dinner for our guests. We used the smaller family kitchen to clean and boil everything in. We also used it to hang our wet clothes and packs on lines we had strung and tied to the low rafters in the little kitchen. We hoped our guests would appreciate our efforts to avoid catching the sickness by using Henry's time-tested advice and experience.

We were just about ready when one of the Abenaki warriors came in from replenishing the firewood and informed us our guests had arrived. We had cooked all their favorite foods and hoped they would enjoy the wine we were able to buy for the event.

Father Neel said the house had never been so full of humanity in all the times he had visited it. He and Father Donne made an inspection tour and marveled at our washroom operation.

"You are really serious about avoiding the sicknesses, aren't you, Yancy?" remarked Father Donne.

"Yes we are."

We all sat on benches around the huge, solid maple table. Although the house wasn't built for an upper-class family, it still had character driven mostly by its hardwood doors, window casings, and furniture. Maple wasn't the only wood used. Cherry had been used for the cabinets and benches in the smaller family kitchen.

Fathers Neel and Donne were the only ones who drank any wine, I noticed, although I had a sip. It was too bitter for me, as it was for the warriors and for Yancy. Henry had trained Yancy and me to serve hot turkey broth if there was any sickness in the area. Everyone except the priests had cups of hot broth with the meal.

"Please bring us up to date on all the news and gossip," I requested of our guests.

Father Donne spoke up first. "There are more than seven hundred people and one hundred homes and businesses and church buildings in the city as of the last count, and it is still growing. More than a third of the people living in the city are priests, nuns, or Jesuits. We as a faith are committed to winning souls and helping the needy."

Father Neel added, "The city has had a tough fall with a lot of the Indians living in and near the city getting sick. In prior years, we had a few people come down with lung infections or serious colds, but this year the number of sick Indians is enormous. Remember, we only see the sick in the city, but we hear terrible stories about the sicknesses in some of the northern villages. Many of the smaller villages and bands have been hit so hard with sickness and deaths that survivors are merging with others bands and villages.

"We focus, as you do, on personal hygiene and turkey broths. We use the secretion from beaver glands to reduce fevers and inflammation, and we use vinegar to cool and cleanse their skins, and anything else we can find to help them. Sometimes, however, nothing helps. The thing that discourages us the most is that the more social interaction there is with the Indians, more of them seem to get sick. We want to help them and witness to them. At the same time, we don't want to infect them with whatever someone seems to be carrying."

Yancy decided to change the subject so the Abenaki warriors wouldn't get too frightened. He asked about any changes in the fur-trading business. Father Neel mentioned he had seen two trappers leading horses loaded with furs, so he checked with the trading post. They told him this was the first year they had seen anyone use horses, and the horses did well. Yancy and I looked at each other and smiled.

Father Donne mentioned to us that the government agents weren't enforcing the king's laws as stringently as they had in the past—especially relating to only Catholics buying property in New France—because of the diminished supply of beaver pelts being sold to the trading posts. "It's astounding, isn't it, how money changes political priorities?" I commented.

"You're more right than you think, Zoel," Father Donne remarked.

"You're a Catholic, right, Zoel?"

"Sorry, Father, but I'm not." There was utter silence.

Yancy jumped in for a second time in an effort to get

things back on track. "What's new outside of Quebec City, Father?"

"Cod fishing at the mouth of the St. Lawrence and up and down the Atlantic coast is becoming a major battleground between the French, English, and a number of other European countries. You know that cod fish is a non-oily fish and with a little cheap salt dries quickly in the sun and can be kept for years. With this advantage, all the countries are fishing, and there are battles brewing all the time. Europeans have always had a taste for cod; and with salt being so cheap now, everyone is fishing for cod. It could bring some of the countries to war soon."

I gave our guests Henry's and Josh's mail for France and asked if they had any mail for us. "None yet," Father Donne replied. I was disappointed my grandfather hadn't written again, but that wouldn't stop me from writing to him before spring.

"With sickness around, do you think we should stay here for the winter?" I asked.

They shared a quick glance and then Father Neel said, "You are here alone and in your own home. We think you are safe. But we suggest you don't mingle with the local Indians or spend much time in the city. Keep in mind, almost half of the Indians we saw died of venereal diseases. If you can be comfortable in this home and the surrounding areas, we think you'll be fine."

We all looked at one another. I knew no one was very happy with his answer. Keeping ourselves locked up in a big house for the winter was not what we had anticipated as a fun time in Quebec City. The dinner was over; but before leaving, Father Neel asked to pray with us. In his prayer for us was a request for Godly wisdom regarding our plans for the winter and for protection in our decision. He sensed our unhappiness. I was glad he had prayed for us because I sensed we were going to need it.

The supper had been a success. After our guests left, I thanked everyone for his contribution. The clean-up process was slow as we scrubbed everything with vinegar and boiled all our utensils before we put them away. The Abenaki warriors gathered together before they went to bed. Yancy and I left them alone.

CHAPTER 11

Safe in the Snow

We all got up early—long before sunrise. The warriors informed us, "We have decided to go home because it's too risky for us to stay here for the winter."

Yancy said it for me, "Where you go, we go!"

They were surprised and pleased. I said, "We are family and we will travel home with you *after* we prepare properly, okay? Let's sit down and begin planning." They all joined me at the big table; I took out my pen, ink, and paper.

"We need to leave today," one of the warriors said anxiously.

"What if we hit a three-day snowstorm and the snow is four feet deep?" I asked him.

"We will all die," another quickly replied.

"You're right. So why not plan for the worst and be ready for the storm and the snow?" After a minute or so, they were all in agreement. The first thing I wrote on my list and mentioned to them was getting snowshoes. That brought smiles, and the tone in the room changed. Someone mentioned gloves, another mentioned hats and warmer coats. The list grew to include light wood to start fires, extra flints, extra buckskins for wigwams, and extra food, and so forth.

The list was done just as daylight broke. We heated up some breakfast. Everyone's mood was positive. "I'll take this list to the trapper's store and get them working on it as well as on Josh's and Henry's lists. How about the items you each want to buy? Can we make a list of them, or do you want to shop for them when we pick up the rest of the supplies?"

Everyone wanted to shop for his own items, which made it easier on me. I told them I would pay for all the extra winter equipment. I wanted us to carry a limited amount of light trade goods home with us and asked if that would be all right with them. They all understood and indicated they were fine with that.

I was ready to head out to place our orders. I wanted everything ready for pickup by the middle of the afternoon. They could shop for their personal items then. But before we could leave, I reminded them that the place had to be cleaned and the firewood replaced. The warriors volunteered to clean it and to cut and stack firewood as well as get the packs and their items ready to go. Yancy mentioned he needed to visit his friends to make sure they were all set for the winter. He said he'd be back before lunch though. We headed out together. As we walked down the road, he turned to me and said, "You did great, Zoel. You reminded me of Henry today—putting the family's safety first." I thanked him for his compliment; then we parted at the street corner.

With the orders placed, I decided to stop at the church and bring our friends up to date. They weren't surprised and complimented us on our decision and preparations. I gave them the rent money and some silver for whatever they needed. Just as I was getting ready to say good-bye, Father Neel reached into his desk and pulled out an envelope, which, he said, had arrived early that morning. It was the letter I had been waiting for from my grandfather. It had come in on a ship late the previous evening while we were having supper together. I thanked him and stuck it in my coat pocket. Then I handed him one of the keys to the house and told him I would leave the other one on the kitchen table. I thanked them for their help and left.

The diseases and deaths had saddened the city for me. I assumed it would pass, but I felt compassion for those in the middle of it. I hoped we could leave the diseases behind and not bring them with us to the Abenaki villages.

On my walk back to the house, I reflected on the items I had ordered and went over them in my mind to make sure nothing had been forgotten. I had ordered colorful clothing and a limited number of knives and kitchen silverware and only a few pots, pans, and axes this time. They were just too heavy. For each of us, I found some deerskin-lined canvas coats with hoods—like those used by sailors—plus gloves, hats, snowshoes, and all the other items on the list. Henry's and Josh's lists were easy to fill. It was the same old stuff. I thought ahead to spring. I wondered, *What will I be buying for the horses then?* I was certain Josh would help me with that when the time came.

It was snowing a little as I arrived at the front door. I figured the storm would pass soon, so I wasn't worried about it. When I opened the door, I saw that everyone was busy cleaning. The placed smelled like vinegar. I said to myself, *They are truly my brothers*. I thanked the Lord for each of them and prayed none of us would get sick or pass a sickness on to anyone else. Like them, I couldn't wait to leave town.

I heard Yancy's voice and asked him if all was well. "Yes, everything's fine with my friends; they're set for the winter."

Two hours later, we were on our way to shop and pick up the ordered items. By the time we finished packing and loading them up, it was almost dark. We wore our new jackets and looked like nine bears from the big, bad north woods. But everybody loved them—and the snowshoes. We spent most of the evening after supper repacking and getting ready so we could leave early in the morning. After I finished packing and checking everybody's packs, I decided it was time to sit down in front of the bedroom fireplace and read my grandfather's letter.

He had been shopping for the horses he felt had the best chance of surviving the ocean crossing and the new climate. He had found four he felt were perfect. While checking out the four horses, the stable boy told him he had worked with the horses since their births and wanted to travel to New France with them. The boy was fifteen, he said, and would complete his commitment to his current employer on his sixteenth birthday, which was on December 5th. My grandfather went on to say, "I have met with the boy's employer, the farm owner, and I have received his permission to allow the boy to travel to New France with the four horses. The farmer had taken him in as an orphan and agreed to provide for him if he worked on the farm until he was sixteen."

I couldn't believe it! Not only was he sending me an extra

horse but a caretaker as well. In closing, he encouraged me to accept the lad as a full-time employee in my new venture. He assured me that when he arrived he would have everything he needed, plus the skill with the horses I would need. My grandfather really was my silent, full-time business partner. I had a lot to thank him for and hurried to share the news with Yancy. He was excited and carefully read the letter line by line. He was actually reading my grandfather's written French; it was wonderful to hear him read it aloud.

How could I ever thank my grandfather enough, I wondered? As I lay in bed thinking about everything, I prayed and thanked God for His goodness to me. He overwhelmed me with His gifts. Although I had lost both of my parents in a terrible sickness, God had provided me with a new loving and caring family, plus an extended family in France. I needed to refocus now on the safety of our family and get them home without injury or sickness.

There was a light dusting of snow on the ground when we left the house early the next morning. We all knew we would see lots more before we arrived home. While riding the boat across the St. Lawrence, I realized this was the second time I felt safer leaving the city than being in or near it. How could it be that there was more safety and security in the wilderness than in the heart of a city? It was true our family was safer in the snow than sitting in a large house in the middle of a growing community. Henry had been right all along, and I was continually be reminded how important his wisdom was to our new family's future.

CHAPTER 12

Slow and Steady

It was cool—but not cold—as we hustled through familiar woods and over hills. We used every minute of the day before we stopped at what we considered a safe place to set up for the night—just in case snow was on its way. The safe place included wind protection from the northwest and access to fresh water. With tree branches and our extra deerskins, we built two temporary wigwams. We collected wood and then lit fires for cooking and warmth. Our hot meal included squash, corn, beans, and smoked turkey. We had all agreed to eat two hot meals daily—breakfast and supper. To save time and keep ourselves healthy, we nibbled on smoked venison during the day.

The night sky was somewhat hazy, and the moon was at a quarter. There were very few stars. We took turns staying awake to make sure no one surprised or attacked us. How many nights we would have security was open for discussion; but while we were anywhere near New France, we all felt it was necessary.

Although we made good time during the first three days, the weather, we noticed, was getting colder, and the sky was clouding up. On the evening of the third day, it started to snow just as we began to set up the temporary wigwams. After the wigwams were finished, Yancy asked that everyone collect more firewood and keep piling it up until dark. We were camped in a hollow with water running from a spring in the mountain behind us. We were protected from the northwest wind, but the snow was getting heavier and blowing really hard. We cooked a hot meal again and kept the fires going all night long.

It snowed the entire next day. By the middle of the afternoon, we had about a foot of the white stuff. We collected more firewood and packed as much snow as we could on the windward side of the wigwams to keep the cold wind out. The smoke from the fires was quickly pulled out the other side of the wigwams, so no one was bothered by it. We were ready for whatever it took to survive the storm, and we prayed for God's help and protection from danger. We rotated staying awake during the night—but not just for security reasons this time. We wanted to make sure we were not buried in snow or woke up freezing cold because the fires had gone out. Our new coats, gloves, and hats saved the day—and the night. Everyone slept in his, as did I.

We rationed the food—just in case—and took turns running for water from the spring. We sang songs and everyone got an opportunity to tell stories and jokes. We slept off and on. We stayed there two days and three nights before it stopped snowing. It didn't warm up much, but it was clear and sunny. We were rested and ready to use our snowshoes. It was a first for all of us, so it was slow work. We had received about three feet of snow, but there were huge drifts and then open areas of no snow at all. Put the snowshoes on and then take them off was our routine for two more days. We were not able to cover more than ten miles each day.

We noticed the snow was getting deeper with fewer bare patches of ground. We also realized we had not received the worst of the storm where we had camped. We were now walking through four feet of snow and much deeper drifts. Knowing we had been blessed, we didn't complain and were able to crank it up a notch now that we knew how to use the snowshoes.

Days later when we figured we were fewer than seventy-five miles from home, I asked Yancy if we should kill a deer and resupply our smoked venison and maybe clean up a little. He reminded me that we were near the lake that we had to go around during one of our earlier trips. We shared our plans with everyone and then camped early near the lake. Yancy and one of the warriors headed out to kill a buck. The rest of us set up the temporary wigwams, started fires, and built a larger fire to cook and smoke the deer outside. We thought we heard the sound of Yancy's musket. We kept busy and impatiently waited for them to return to camp.

An hour passed before we saw them coming. What they were hauling didn't look like a deer. As they got closer, we saw that what was hanging on a long pole was a mountain lion with a big hole in its neck. It was beautiful! Everyone had lots of questions, which were asked and answered while we skinned, sliced, and cooked the cat for supper. We ate the ribs and back steaks; they had an unusual taste. After supper we smoked the quarters, and Yancy retold the story—beginning to end.

"We were watching two bucks banging horns and making all kinds of noises. The bucks were going at each other pretty heavily, so we were watching the fight. Then I noticed a lion crawling along the snow on a ledge. I figured it would jump on the losing buck after the fight was over. To make sure we got the deer meat we needed, the warrior fired his arrow at one of the bucks. He missed, however, and the lion leaped on the back of the nearest buck. I aimed and fired my musket at the same buck, trying to hit his heart, but the lion took the bullet in its neck. The bucks fled the scene, and we got the lion by default." Everyone loved his story.

Yancy took his time preparing and cleaning what he wanted to keep, such as the skin, fangs, teeth, ears, and tail. It had been an unusual afternoon and evening—and a fun break.

The quarters smoked late into the night and then cooled quickly in the freezing air. In the morning, we wrapped them in deerskins, packed them in our backpacks, cleaned the campsite, and headed for home.

We encountered two more snowstorms. But they were nothing like the first one, and they only delayed us an additional two days. The going never got much faster than twelve miles a day because most of the time we were on snowshoes—and glad to have them. We stopped off and picked up our canoes in the small village along the river. We cut two poles and ran them down the sides of each canoe. Tying the poles to the canoes allowed two people—one in the front and one in the rear—to grab the poles and easily tote the canoes. Those doing the toting put their backpacks inside them, and the rest of us relieved them periodically. We didn't have a long way to go, and walking was safer than being on the half-frozen river.

One miracle of our trip was that no one became sick—not even with a cold. The startled looks on some of the villagers' faces when they saw us carrying our three canoes loaded with backpacks; wearing our heavy, hooded coats; and walking on snowshoes convinced us they thought we were from another land—that is, until they looked under our hoods. Once we were recognized, others came out of their wigwams, laughing and cheering. They had never seen jackets with hoods like ours, and they had never seen snowshoes. We put the canoes down, took off our snowshoes, and danced around with some of them. Others gave us hugs. It felt so good to be back in our healthy Abenaki village. Everyone knew our safe arrival had been a miracle.

CHAPTER 13

Managing Fear

Peter, Nadie, Anna, and Henry made our winter. At their insistence, Yancy and I moved into their wigwam. Henry said he wouldn't hear of us spending the winter anywhere else. It was the best thing Yancy and I could have done to make the winter enjoyable, comfortable, and educational.

There was no celebration supper on our return. It was too cold and the snowstorms too many. At Henry's request, we visited with the chief and the village council and shared some of what it was like to have survived the storms. Some of the warriors shared what they had seen as well.

We were careful, however, not to share too much about the sickness because it would have been self-defeating. The warriors talked enough about it to kindle fear in many, so Yancy and I tried to focus on the positives of what we did to protect ourselves to make sure everyone came home healthy. Henry shared what he had learned about the risks of not intelligently managing the food preparation process, the kinds of food we all needed to eat, the correct sanitation processes we needed to follow, and what he felt helped to keep us from acquiring the infectious diseases. The council members asked a lot of questions and thanked us for sharing what we had learned and our concerns. As we walked from the meeting, I had a distinct feeling we would hear more from the chief on the subject.

During the first week of our return, the seven warriors who had traveled with us were treated as celebrities because of their unique warm clothing and snowshoes. My friend the canoe builder offered to make snowshoes for anyone who was willing to trade for them. It didn't take long before he, his family, and fellow craftsmen had a whole new group of customers.

The snow came and went all winter long. It never got more than three feet deep, and at times there was none on the ground. We used the days when it didn't snow to hunt for food, repair the wigwams, and replace the firewood we had used. The days and nights were still cold—with or without snow. We were all careful to stay hydrated and fueled with Henry's hot soups and Anna's cooking.

All the weddings had taken place while we were away. Josh was beside himself with happiness. His wife, Adoette (big tree), was a little shorter than he and slender, but she was a very strong woman. Her parents were excellent examples of good health. They were pleased with the marriage and mainly because Josh had a reputation for caring for others and especially for Indians like Yancy. The four of them—living together in her parents' wigwam—were getting along well. Josh had snowshoes made for himself and for Adoette; and on good winter days, they trapped beaver and fox together. Josh shared that Adoette was looking forward to traveling with him anywhere he needed to go.

Anna shared that Sooleawa was happy with her new family and suggested I stop by and visit them as soon as possible. When I told her I needed to think about it, she just laughed and said, "You haven't changed, Zoel."

I did run into Sooleawa a few days later. We stopped and chatted for a while. She was beaming with joy and said she loved being a wife and mother. I told her I couldn't be happier for her.

*   *   *

Henry, in addition to teaching his French classes, put together a series of lessons on the old books of the Bible. He said everybody loved the Old Testament stories, he thought, because there was so much action in them. The number of attendees was diminishing, he mentioned, and thought he knew why: The meeting we had with the chief just after the team returned disturbed many of the council members. They were concerned about catching diseases from us. I asked him if we should meet with them again and clarify what we are doing that is different to prevent that from happening. He suggested we may just need to let sleeping dogs lie.

When it wasn't snowing, Yancy and I, with snowshoes on and muskets in hand, went hunting. We shared all of what we killed and cleaned, but we noticed some of the warriors were not as friendly to us as they had been in the past. I talked with Yancy about the storm I saw brewing. He said, "The best way to avoid paranoia in the village is to meet with the chief alone and find out what their issues are and what they want us to do about them."

I pushed Henry for a meeting with the chief. He was opposed to it. His response was, "I don't like it, but I will set it up."

No gifts, no food, just a face-to-face meeting, I figured, would help get to the issues quickly. Yancy liked my approach. But I knew Henry was much too smooth to do that, so I suggested he not attend. He happily agreed. Just the chief, Yancy, and I would be meeting together.

We met in his wigwam where his wife served hot soup. It was pepper-hot not just fireplace-hot soup. Yancy loved it and told her so. The chief asked me what was on our minds. I asked him, "Do you know why many of the warriors and council members have distanced themselves from Yancy and me?"

He smiled. "Honest and a good question. You have frightened everyone because you travel so much to Quebec City to make money. By doing so, they are afraid you will make everyone in the village sick. They think you are no longer a friend or you wouldn't put them and their families at risk. If you tell them you will no longer go to 'sick city,' they will be relieved and continue to be your friends."

He nailed me. I had four horses and a groomsman arriving in the spring. I had to go back to what he called sick city to pick them up. I responded by reviewing all that Yancy and I had done to avoid bringing the disease to the village.

"No one is saying you don't care and haven't worked hard to reduce risk. They are just saying you care more about money than you care about their families and their health.

Let me make it easy for you, Zoel. Anyone who goes to or near Quebec City from now on can no longer return to this village."

"I appreciate your straightforwardness, chief."

"What are you going to do in the spring, Zoel?"

"I have horses and a groomsman arriving from France then. Yancy and I will pick them up in the city."

"I understand you have to honor prior commitments, and I feel bad that you cannot return to the village, but it appears that's what's best for the village."

He asked more questions about our supper conversation with Fathers Neel and Donne and if anyone had determined how to avoid the diseases. I told him no one had yet, but eliminating sex between the Indians and the Europeans might eliminate half the deaths. He then turned to Yancy. "Have you traveled west to the large lakes?"

"No, not all the way to the lakes, but I have talked to a few who have."

"Would being near and on the lakes be a healthy place to live?"

"I hear they have more snowstorms than we have here, but other than that life is good there."

He thanked us for being candid. He said he and Henry would meet later and talk some more.

We headed back to our wigwam. I felt sad. I had never thought of myself as a greedy, bad guy before. We immediately shared everything with Henry. He looked at me, shook his head, and said, "I know you love them and would never put any of them at risk. However, they only feel fear, and fear doesn't come from God. It comes from the devil. The devil is trying to chase us out of here because we are trying to do God's work by healing the spiritually and physically sick. You are the ones who make it possible by traveling back and forth to Quebec City."

"I think they are going to move west, Henry."

He looked surprised. "Do *you* think so, Yancy?"

"Yes, I agree with Zoel. And I also think the chief intentionally let us know they will be moving out in the spring so we could make our plans."

"He is a courageous and smart chief," Henry remarked.

"What if we lay out our plans for him in detail so he can predict for the council and the rest of the villagers that we will no longer create any disease risk for them?" I asked.

"How would we do that?" Yancy questioned.

"I suggest that you, Henry, confirm to the chief that Yancy and I will head to sick city as soon as we trap and trade for a few more furs and the winter weather backs off a little—and that we won't be back. That will take the pressure off him and the council. Then, with Josh's help and help from the seven braves who traveled with Yancy and me, you take our family to a new temporary home farther down the river. You pay the braves with some of the remaining trade goods. We'll take the horses, which will be carrying the new supplies, east of the village and meet you farther down the river."

Henry responded—mimicking me—"I need to think about that." We all laughed.

Later in the week, Henry met with the chief and the council. The crisis was over after they reviewed our plans to leave. With the help of the seven single warriors, we would all be gone at the arrival of spring. Word traveled fast; the warriors were at our wigwam wanting to choose their payments *now* before the top trade goods were gone. It was a joy for Yancy and me to help them find the best of what we had. We knew how heavy Henry's books were and how much work it was going to be to move him, his family, and all his belongings.

CHAPTER 14

His Special Gift

Now that everyone in the village knew we were leaving, the smiles were back and all was at peace again. It was obvious the entire village was going to move west later in the spring. Anna was not happy about pulling up stakes, but she was looking forward to finding a permanent home somewhere farther down the Connecticut River.

Peter was becoming Henry's right-hand man. I was amazed at how he was growing in knowledge and patience. He still hadn't accepted Jesus as his Savior, but he was no longer bitter and truly loved his new family. Nadie was walking and talking in multiple, confusing languages. It was great to spend the winter with them. Yancy enjoyed them as much as I did. He said he felt like an uncle; I told him I understood. It was getting close to travel time for us. I knew I would miss the family while I was gone.

Warm breezes were melting the remaining snow; frequent rain showers were filling the river and our little creek. Yancy and I decided we'd take our hooded coats and snowshoes with us just in case we had a spring snowstorm. We both knew the spring snowstorms were the most dangerous because of the high-water content in the snow. Two feet of wet snow could freeze at night and kill us. Almost all the trade goods were gone again. Our two packs were loaded with beaver and fox skins as well as some deerskins for a temporary wigwam. We said our good-byes to everyone we knew in the village. We had grown to love many of the Abenaki villagers, and they obviously felt the same. We could see love and, at the same time, relief in their eyes as we parted company for the last time.

They had been good to us, and we had been good to them. None of them had come down with any unusual sicknesses while we were their guests, and we had provided them with lots of equipment, clothing, and medicinal items that materially improved their quality of life. Most important, some of them had accepted Jesus as their Savior and knew Him well enough to continue to tell others about Him. Henry had been blessed in his French classes. Knowing that only the Holy Spirit can open one's heart, we were thankful for His work in the hearts of some of the Abenaki villagers.

*   *   *

The walk to Quebec City wasn't as much fun with just the two of us, but it was faster. Yancy and I ate hot meals twice a day—for health reasons—but ate little during the day. We found if we focused on safety first and speed second, we could cover a lot of ground in one day. I loved Yancy as a brother and admired his stamina. He took the lead at times and at other times I did. The key was to give up the lead if we weren't crisp and wide awake because a surprise—particularly in the form of robbers or a bear—could kill us.

We spotted a band of Indians before they spotted us and hid until they passed. They didn't look like trouble, especially since they had young braves with them. They looked as though they were just out hunting. We also spotted two Frenchmen with muskets headed east; but because we couldn't tell what they were carrying, we didn't know if they were traders or trappers. In the shortest time ever, we were at the river. It felt great to be getting my body into the conditioned shape it was designed to be in. The river was high. Yancy said the water would be within four or five feet of the floor of his boat repair barn. He was looking forward to seeing how the business had progressed over the winter for both him and Josh. I enjoyed being on a boat again. It felt good. With the deeper water and heavier current, the crossing was a little tougher for the men paddling and steering.

Once ashore, we headed immediately to the trading post and sold our furs and completed our partnership financial transactions. We couldn't order any trade goods until we determined what the horses could carry. The associate at the trading post said the horses had arrived with their caretaker and were temporarily staying at a farm just past the church. The caretaker had rented the place until we arrived. He also told us everything had gone well on the trip, and many in the town were thrilled to see the horses. The caretaker, he said, had hired a boot maker to begin making packs for the horses so they could carry trade goods and furs. Yancy and I were delighted and impressed and looked forward to meeting our new caretaker. To me the word *caretaker* was special, and I thought of Yancy and myself as caretakers of sorts.

We headed for the church and met with Father Neel and Father Donne. They were excited for us because they had seen the horses and met the caretaker. They told us we would be pleasantly surprised. They also shared about their tough winter with too many sicknesses and too many deaths. They were still caring for a lot of ill people, so we passed on their invitation to stay there. We gave them tithes from each of the partners; they thanked us as usual. I suggested we do the same thing we had done on the previous trip: have supper together tomorrow night at the farm. They were pleased with that. We had just enough time—that is, if we hustled—to get to the farm before dark.

The farm was small and the building was more of a barn than a house. The horses were grazing and wore halters with long ropes tied to small trees. As we walked up, we saw two men making something with leather and a wood frame. The younger one said, "You're Zoel," and reached out his hand. He was a good-looking, young man about my size with a great smile.

"Yes, I'm Zoel. And this is my partner Yancy."

Yancy gave him a good handshake and then Leon Durand introduced us to the boot maker and described to us what they were making.

The pack they were making was a lined leather one that would allow us to haul almost anything we chose to without hurting the horse. The pack would sit on the horse's back and be tied under its belly like a saddle. The loaded pack would have to be evenly balanced. It was designed to open on both sides to hold beaver skins or to be closed to hold trading goods. It looked practical. It had multiple layers of leather sewed together to make it strong, yet it was still flexible and would be comfortable and easy on the horse's back. Leon said there would be a blanket, which we would change and clean often, under the pack to keep the horse's skin healthy.

Leon had used similar packs to haul farm goods to his town market in France. They had already made two and had at least four more to go. He walked us over and introduced us to the horses, which actually had walked up to him before we got to them. It was obvious they liked and trusted him, or he had something sweet for them. He gave them no reward; we were impressed.

"Do they ever run off on you?" I asked.

"Not unless they get spooked, and then they just come back," he replied.

For some reason, I didn't expect the horses to be as well trained. Neither did I expect Leon Durand to be a professional horse manager. Grandpa had truly done well.

There was space in the building for the three of us to stay. Leon had rented it and placed a deposit on it, which I reimbursed him for. Yancy and I prepared supper after settling in. From our discussions both during and after supper, we discovered much of what we needed to know about each other. I asked, "Leon, what are your expectations?"

"I hope to work for you in your trapping and trading business. But I know I have little to offer and lots to learn." Yancy and I shared a glance acknowledging we got the right man with the right attitude.

Leon and his boot maker worked the next day on making

more packs. Yancy and I headed to the trapper's store. We placed our orders for Josh, Henry, and ourselves, plus a long list of trading goods now that we knew it was the horses that would be doing the toting. I asked Yancy what he thought we should order for Leon. He said, "A custom musket and all that goes with it, a hooded coat, a pair of gloves, a hat like ours, and a good skinning knife. You know he will want them once we are in the wild." Between the trapper's store and the musket maker's shop, we ordered everything we thought he would need for the next year.

For all three of us, the next two weeks were filled with learning new things. Yancy and I learned how to handle the horses and pack and unpack their totes. Leon learned how to load and fire a musket and ended up being a good shot. He practiced with mine and requested the horses' presence during the firing of the weapons. He said they learn quickly as long as those taking care of them don't panic.

Leon had multiple bridles made for the horses as well as backup packs in case any were damaged or stolen. We ate all our meals at home and stayed away from the church mission and any gathering places in town. We spent evenings planning and making lists of things we needed to do just to make sure we didn't forget anything.

Grandpa had sent a letter with Leon in which he wished us the best and asked lots of questions about New France. I realized he really wanted to come but felt he was too old and didn't want to be a burden. He had done so much for us, and I didn't know how to thank him. Henry told me many times that sharing what was on my heart was my best witness and to let the Holy Spirit do the rest. So, that's what I did. I wrote to my grandfather and just shared with him what was on my heart.

Every day that passed, Yancy and I were more impressed with Leon and his ability to manage the horses. They weren't nervous or high-strung horses like those I remembered seeing in France. Leon's musket finally arrived with cleaning tools, powder horn, extra balls, and flints. Having noticed on our last trip how much Yancy liked his musket cover, I bought two more: one to protect Leon's musket and one to protect my musket.

I asked Yancy what he thought about teaching Leon to speak and write in Nipmuck during our trip. He thought it was a good idea. I asked Fathers Neel and Donne if they could help me find a copy of Henry's Nipmuck-French language translation documents. I knew Henry had shared the documents with them as well as with many others. I also asked if they knew where I could buy some French books. They said they would do their best to find out. I was optimistic they would find what we needed to bring Leon Durand, God's special gift, up to speed.

They took pride in what they built.
Courtesy of Jack Mann

CHAPTER 15

Light Reading

Time for leaving was soon approaching. We were heading for new territory, which excited me. During the next few days, we cashed out all our partners' accounts and converted our certificates to gold and silver, using the power of attorney documents Josh and Henry had provided before we left. With multiple trading posts up and down the river now, and with our moving farther away, it was possible three of the four of us may never return to Quebec City. Yancy was committed to return, but he said, "I won't be doing it forever, and Josh helping his buddy in the boat repair business wouldn't go on forever either." I mailed my letter to my grandfather, and then we began cleaning up the rental farm building in preparation for leaving.

We scheduled our last supper of this trip with Father Neel and Father Donne. Since it wasn't Friday, we prepared tender steaks with fruit salad and beans. We also served wine and some small sweet cakes Yancy had picked up at the trapper's store.

Father Donne mentioned to us at supper that most of the horses he had seen in France had "docked" tails, and he was surprised that the tails of the stallion and the three mares were long. Leon explained that the farm he was indentured to was a vegetable farm. He believed the excessive number of flies on the farm was the reason why the owner didn't cut any of his horses' tails, which he said delighted him. He said the farmer was not a loving man like he thought a dad should be, but he was always practical and most of the time kind.

Father Donne shared about a visit they'd had with a priest from Montreal. Their guest talked a lot about their fur-trading post, which had been established in 1611 by Samuel de Champlain, and how it had grown beyond anyone's dreams.

Yancy shared with them that many of the Abenaki villages were planning to move west to avoid the sickness that had swept through the eastern villages during the winter. Father Neel mentioned he had heard the French government was encouraging many of the Indians, and specifically the very large Iroquois-Mohawk tribe, to move farther west and north to make way for more French settlements. It was obvious to all of us everything was changing along the St. Lawrence River as more Europeans headed across the Atlantic for a new start.

The horses continually became the subject of conversation. Leon was put on the hot seat many times and always did well. Father Neel asked how much the four horses could carry. Leon responded, "It depends on how far they must travel and the type of terrain. They can usually carry the weight of a normal man for many hours with reasonable rest and food. I suggest we travel with three loaded horses, giving one a break and then rotating breaks so we never have to stop for very long periods of time." Leon had their attention. Yancy and I were delighted.

While we were eating the sweet cakes, Father Donne handed me two packages. "These two gifts are for you, Zoel; we hope you'll enjoy them."

In the first package was a copy of Henry's document recording Nipmuck words and then translating the sound and meaning of each into French. He said one of the ladies in their church had handwritten a copy for me; I commented on her writing. It was lovely. In a separate package was a book called *The Fifteen Joys of Marriage*, published between 1480 and 1490. Father Donne said it was a riotous critique of wives and thought we might enjoy reading it. He also said it provided an accurate description of family living in France in the previous century. I thought, *What an excellent book to use to teach Leon how to write. Having lived there, he will relate to some of it.*

The evening went fast and was a lot of fun for each of us. Leon enjoyed the banter and sharing and had impressed both priests. Before they left, Father Neel prayed for our safety and asked the Lord to bring us back to them soon. He also prayed for Leon and asked the Lord to make his new home a sweet and safe place to live. After saying our good-byes, we cleaned up and finished packing. Our plan was to leave at sunrise. We slept well. I dreamt of beautiful white-topped mountains and a large lake. After waking up, I was surprised at my dream because it was the dream Henry had told me he kept having.

* * *

We packed the horses as Leon had suggested, leaving one of the mares without a load. Each of us carried light food, clothing packs, weapons, and snowshoes. It was great not having to tote trading goods. I could visualize walking all day with little stress.

The horses had no problem riding the large boats across the river. Leon said he didn't think they would ever be bothered by boats after the turbulent ocean crossing. We headed more south this time and looked for a new trail that had been described to us at the trading post. It included more mountains; but we had been told the trails were good, and the streams in the summer were safe to cross. The first day's travel was different. Yancy and I each led a mare. Leon led the stallion with a mare's lead line tied to the stallion's pack. It took me most of the day to adjust to leading a horse. As the day passed, I realized I was most comfortable when the horse and I walked together with no pressure on the lead line. Leon said, "As time passes, you will seldom feel any pressure on the line because the horse will adapt to your walking pace."

Our first night's stop was completely different. We spent the first part of the evening settling down in an area where the horses could graze—that is, after we removed their packs, brushed them down, and gave them water. We had given each horse a break from carrying packs during the day. We found the easiest way to unload one horse and load another was for one of us to hold the receiving horse still while the other two of us lifted the packs from the tired horse and immediately tied them down on the receiving horse.

The second and third days were interesting as we got to know the horses more. We took turns leading each horse.

Leon suggested we rotate so the horses would get comfortable with each of us as quickly as possible. The stallion was a little more sensitive to hand movements than the mares, I noticed, but other than that none of them were any problem. In fact, I enjoyed receiving occasional nuzzles from them. My new life with horses was exciting. I had no idea what was in store for us. I just took it as it came.

After we climbed a small hill, we saw a small band of Abenaki warriors with their families walking toward us. There were about two dozen people in all. We stopped and chatted and learned they were on their way to visit friends in another village. After chatting about the weather and the beautiful mountains, they told us they had seen two horses a few months before. Then they asked if they could pet ours. It was good to know there were other horses in the area; maybe we would run into them.

Seventy miles south and a little east of Quebec City, a range of mountains miles far off in the distance came into view. Although it was summer, a small amount of snow still remained on them. We made very good time, and Leon was doing well. After a week of travel, we decided to take a break and stopped in a small valley near a stream with lots of grazing opportunity. Late in the afternoon, a terrific thunder and lightning storm occurred. The horses didn't get spooked, which surprised me. While the storm was doing its thing, they just stood there silently—not grazing or moving at all—waiting for it to end. *Amazing!*

One evening in our temporary wigwam, I began reading my new book. It was funny and my laughter attracted Leon's attention. He asked me what was funny. I read him the two paragraphs that had made me laugh. He, too, thought they were hilarious.

"You know I can read some French, Zoel, but not a lot. I can read and understand numbers because it was part of my job to take groceries to market and sell them."

"Would you like to learn more?"

"Yes ... definitely yes!"

I motioned for him to sit next to me. I pointed at each word in the first paragraph as I read it. Then he pointed to each word as he tried to read it. He knew a few of the words, and we stumbled through the rest.

Every night of the following week, we did the same thing. Then one night, Yancy showed Leon how well he could read French. They read a paragraph together as Leon and I had. Pleased with themselves, they laughed when finished. Yancy had just the right temperament with people. You knew he cared when he talked, and you couldn't avoid his comfortable nature. I was convinced Leon would know how to read and write French before he realized it. Yancy and I agreed to talk French during our travels to make it easier on him. Once he had mastered reading and writing French, we committed to get him involved in Nipmuck.

CHAPTER 16

Abenaki Two

The White Mountains were close enough to touch as we headed west toward the Connecticut Lakes and south toward the river. We were now in familiar territory, Yancy said, because he had trapped this area right after we first arrived at the Abenaki village. He pointed to two small ponds where he and Josh had trapped a half dozen beaver. We noticed some warriors fishing the larger pond. They waved. It looked as if one of them was in the process of catching a large fish.

Our plan was to follow the river south until we found the village where Henry and Josh were staying. The summer weather was hot and humid. But with the horses carrying most of the weight now, it was so much easier. Our evening studies were going well, and we weren't in a big hurry. We shot turkeys more often than deer for two reasons: they were easier to shoot with muskets than with bows and arrows, and they were easier to clean and prepare for eating. Henry thought turkey meat was better for our health anyway. His opinion was based mainly on his observation that there was less fat in it. I enjoyed the distinct, sweet taste of dark turkey meat, and I liked it in stews and soups.

*   *   *

The Connecticut River was a welcomed sight, but traveling too close to it was impractical because of heavy vegetation. We took the higher ground and looked forward to arriving at the next Indian village. We hadn't trapped any beaver on our trip so far. We didn't feel we had time to, considering Henry and the rest of the family had planned to move out of the Abenaki village soon after we left.

Leon noticed a small group of Indians in canoes on the river. They were too far away for us to recognize, but I suspected we were close to a village. A couple miles farther down, we saw a village with its wigwams covering most of the small valley as it sloped to the river. We approached cautiously, our weapons ready but still strapped over our shoulders rather than by our sides.

The first Abenaki villager we ran into was a young brave. We unintentionally caught him by surprise. He looked at the horses and then ran off toward the wigwams screaming in Abenaki-Penobscot. Many of the warriors came running toward us with their bows loaded. Behind them was Josh, who was trying to settle them down, but it wasn't working. The warriors circled around us but stayed away from the horses. None of them shot their arrows, but we could see they were ready to. But once the chief got their attention, they settled down. Henry and the rest of the family were now headed our way; it appeared the danger had passed.

The chief walked toward me and smiled. Henry had prepared him for the horses, so when he got close I petted the face of the horse I was leading. The chief did the same. His action welcomed us to the village. From then on, the horses were everybody's friend.

It wasn't the kind of welcome we had anticipated, but it worked out okay. Everyone in the family was healthy and living in new wigwams built with the help of the villagers. We unloaded the horses. I gave the chief a skinning knife with a sheath, but not before I made sure Henry hadn't already given him one.

We found some grazing grass near the vegetable gardens. After letting the horses drink in the river, we led them to it. We traded lead ropes for long, grazing ropes. We brushed them down and then set them free to eat and rest. There were a lot of village children watching everything we did with the horses. But when we settled down to making our temporary wigwams near the trees, they hustled off to have more fun elsewhere. The family joined us in setting up camp. It was great to be with them again. We were separated from the village a little, so we were able to talk plainly.

Josh told us, "The village hasn't trapped many beaver, but they have a few bear skins and many fox skins they want to trade."

"Some of the warriors know where there are lots of beaver and are more than interested in trapping them," Henry added.

I mentioned to Henry my dream about a large lake near the snow-capped mountains. This excited him, so he asked me all about it. Anna, Peter, and Nadie were excited about the horses and were petting them as they grazed. Adoette and Josh looked happy together and, with Leon's help, were putting together one of the temporary wigwams. Adoette spoke French to Leon, which amazed me. *She must be a quick learner.* We started a fire in a small pit. Within an hour, we were sitting down together enjoying a meal and more conversation. Peter told us he was doing well with his new Indian language and shared some of it with us. He seemed relaxed and comfortable with his new family. Nadie could talk a mile a minute. Every once in a while, I actually understood what she said.

We shared everything we could remember about our visit to Quebec City, including Father Neel's and Father Donne's thanks to everyone for their tithes and that they wanted to be remembered to them. Yancy updated everyone on his and Josh's investments. I added what he didn't say about his help to Chepi's extended family and the six young, orphaned girls.

Josh suggested we plan to stay through the winter and help the villagers earn their trade goods by trapping beaver. He believed there was enough beaver in the area to keep us all busy for the season. After that, we could move on in the spring. Most were comfortable with his plan. Yancy and I looked at each other and just smiled. I knew in my heart we weren't going to spend the winter in the village. The look on Yancy's face said the same.

The summer passed quickly. Henry held his French and Bible teaching classes; Anna and Nadie helped him by encouraging their new friends to attend; Adoette helped Josh trade and trap, as did Yancy and I; and Peter joined Yancy and me in trapping and preparing the beaver pelts for eventual travel. He was growing up and had tons of energy. Leon took care of the horses. And after a fashion, he got involved in trading with the villagers. His experience selling vegetables in the French market made him a natural trader—that is, once he became comfortable with some of the Abenaki-Penobscot words and the value of the trade goods and some of the skins, which didn't take him long.

Our family business was maturing, and Henry and Anna's missionary work was prospering. Although Yancy, Leon, and I slept apart from the village and our family, occasionally Peter came out and spent the night with us. He was becoming a brother; I enjoyed that. There wasn't anything he didn't seem to enjoy doing, including the rotten job of cleaning the beaver skins. Peter and Leon hit it off and had the lack of knowing Nipmuck in common. Peter had started learning Abenaki-Penobscot and said it was a lot like Nipmuck. They would need help, so Yancy and I committed to help them both learn. New languages were an ongoing challenge in the trapping and trading business, just as it was in the missionary work.

I remembered a number of Bible lessons Henry had shared with us. He was focused on how important education was to each of us. He had said, "The difference between a fool and an educated person is that the educated person acknowledges God and His greatness and then trusts God to lead him or her through the rest of his or her life. And honoring God by tithing is one of the signs a believer is maturing in his or her walk and fellowship with God." He always backed his teachings with Scripture verses.

"The fool hath said in his heart, *There is* no God" (Psalms 14:1).

"The fear of the Lord *is* the beginning of knowledge: *but* fools despise wisdom and instruction" (Proverbs 1:7).

"Trust in the Lord with all of thine heart; and lean not unto thine own understandings. In all thy ways acknowledge him, and he shall direct thy paths" (Proverbs 3:5-6).

"Honor the Lord with thy substance, and with the first fruits of all thine increase: so shall thy barns be filled with plenty, and thy presses shall burst out with new wine" (Proverbs 3: 9-10).

CHAPTER 17

No Good News

The summer at Abenaki Village Two was filled with work, learning, and fun—in that order. Abenaki Two was not as big a village as Abenaki One, but it was full of characters. The medicine man didn't like Henry's Bible classes and made a big stink at the council meeting. Henry was invited to speak and defend himself. The medicine man tried to link Henry's teachings about Jesus to bad luck, and he promised a terrible winter and much sickness if Henry continued. The chief and the council respected the medicine man and his past services to the sick in the village.

Henry said he would fight for the right of the medicine man to believe and teach what he believed, and he was disappointed the medicine man wouldn't fight for his right to do the same. The chief asked the medicine man why he wouldn't fight for Henry's right to teach what he believed. The medicine man finally said he would, but only for one season, and he wanted full payment for it. Henry offered to give him a killed and cleaned deer every moon plus his friendship; the medicine man was satisfied with that.

Many of the village warriors were out trapping beaver. Before leaving, however, they had targeted specific trade goods, which they asked Leon to reserve for them. Leon told them it was first come, first served. Some of the warriors weren't very happy with that. Nevertheless, Leon stood his ground and kept his musket handy—but hidden. He was tough. I wasn't sure if he had been born that way or had developed toughness while working on the French farm. When Josh and Yancy returned from trapping, I told them I thought it might be wise if one of the three of us stayed in the village with Leon to make certain things didn't get out of hand. We agreed to take turns.

The summer passed quickly, and fall was on us before we knew it. Although the Connecticut River was down, the fishing was still good. Henry liked to fish—but not in a canoe. The gardens were productive with plenty of corn to share. We killed two to three deer each week and gave them to the village as rent payment; it was appreciated. Peter and I went hunting together a number of times. He was becoming a good shot with a bow and arrow. We had a chance to talk a lot. During one conversation, he told me he couldn't remember ever loving his life before. He still missed his parents but got up each morning happy to be alive and adopted by Henry and Anna; and he just loved his little sister, Nadie. He was a new man in my eyes. And in my heart, I believed he was on his way to finding Jesus, even though he may not have realized it.

We traded most of what we had brought with us with the villagers and the two bands of Abenakis that visited the village. Being right on the river appeared to create more awareness that traders were staying in the village. It attracted more customers. Yancy, Leon, and I counted up the amount of furs we had collected and decided we had enough to justify a trip to a trading post. So at supper that evening, Henry announced we were going to haul our furs to market. Peter immediately stood up and said he wanted to go. Anna's face paled. Henry told Peter they would discuss it later. Peter smiled and sat down.

Josh said he wanted to go; but Adoette was with child and had asked him to stay with her, which was what he wanted to do anyway.

Henry looked at me and asked, "Do you need me on the trip, Zoel?"

"No, Henry. I suggest you stay here and manage the chief and the council and keep the medicine man happy." Everyone laughed at that. We all knew who was going and who was staying—that is, except for Peter.

Knowing Peter wants to travel with us, I'm sure glad I don't live in Henry's wigwam. I had mixed emotions about his coming along. On the one hand, I felt he was strong enough and smart enough, but there was always the danger of robbers and sickness. I decided to walk over to Henry's.

I knocked and asked, "May I come in?"

Anna responded, "You never have to ask, Zoel."

She and Henry were sitting down and had obviously been talking. It appeared that Peter, sitting quietly across from Henry, had just been listening to their conversation.

"Henry, What have you decided to do?"

"I haven't decided. I'm not sure yet what to do."

"May I help?" Henry nodded his head yes.

Directing my question to Peter, I asked, "What's on your mind?"

"I think I can help, and I know I'm strong enough so I won't be a burden. I think I would learn a lot about managing horses, and I'm bigger and stronger than any brave in the village. I know Anna is worried about me. I'm sorry, but I need to make a contribution."

"Those are good points, Peter. Four horses could use four leads. Your energy level tells me you would have no problem with the trip. My only concern for you is you getting a disease or our being attacked by robbers."

Anna piped up and said, "I don't want him to go, Zoel."

I told her I understood. I had stayed as long as I felt was appropriate, so I said good night and headed back to the campsite. Yancy and Leon were wrestling with some of the packs. I gave them a hand and then cleaned up. Before going to sleep, I prayed for God to intervene and help Henry, Anna, and Peter make the right decision.

The next day, Anna informed us she had decided to let Peter go with us but only because she could see him as part of our team and knew we would give our lives if we had to in order to protect him. I loved Anna as a mother and as a friend. What she said she meant, and I hoped we wouldn't let her down.

*   *   *

We decided we'd go to Montreal this time. We thought it would be closer than Quebec City, and we hoped there would be less disease and sickness there. We also reflected on the visiting priest's comments to Fathers Neel and Donne about how successful its trading post was. Underlying all our thoughts was the adventure of traveling to a new place. Yancy and I weren't afraid to admit it.

The river's depth was down. Our plan was to cross it at its shallowest point and then head straight for Montreal. Everything we had learned from others about traveling to Montreal convinced us it should be much easier than traveling to Quebec City. We would assume nothing, though, and be careful all the way.

Peter spent the week with us getting ready and working with the horses. He would be a good caretaker, Leon said, because he was a light sleeper and an early riser, and his movements were easy for the horses to predict.

Ready to leave, we said our good-byes and headed up along the bank of the river and crossed it a few miles past the bend where it was the shallowest. The current was quite slow, and it was obvious it dropped off sediment as it slowed down to make the wide turn. With its gravel and sand bottom, it was three feet at its deepest depth. We had actually crossed deeper rivers with the horses just a few months ago.

Yancy had a pretty good feel for the direction we needed to take, and he was aware of the large lake between us and Montreal. We knew we needed to stay north of it. We ran into two bands of Abenaki warriors out hunting for deer and turkeys. They helped by providing directions.

Peter, like the rest of us, took his turn leading each horse. We had decided to talk Nipmuck as much as we could on the trip. If danger occurred, we agreed to revert to French, but we wanted to try and encourage Leon and Peter to first become comfortable with Nipmuck. After that, other Indian languages would be much easier for them. It was a tough start; but they were game, and Yancy made it fun.

Seven days into the trip, we approached a large bay north of Lake Champlain. Yancy had done well in guiding us to the north of the lake, and Peter had proven he had plenty of stamina. We rested along the shore and enjoyed some fishing and a good break.

As we prepared to head out early the next morning, the stallion whinnied several times, which was very unusual. Then we saw Leon's signal. Someone was nearby. We led the horses to a patch of trees. I climbed up one of the maples and looked around. Everyone was quiet; I could hear the light breeze as it blew through the trees.

A little way up the bay, there were at least a dozen warriors and a European with a musket headed our way. I climbed down quickly and shared what I had seen. "They are traveling light, they are armed, and their bows are loaded."

Yancy said, "They have a scout nearby. Take the horses behind that small hill and wait for me. Their scout will follow you, and I will take care of him."

We did what he said and hustled back down the bay a short way and then walked quickly behind the hill. I asked Peter and Leon to keep the horses quiet while I climbed up the back of the hill and watched for the scout and Yancy.

Time passed slowly; nothing happened. I could clearly see the trail we had taken. No one was coming. But down the hill to my right, I saw something move. Then it moved again. It was a warrior bent down and weaving his way through the bushes. I looked back down the trail. Yancy was coming at a run. I waved to him and pointed down the hill. He saw me and understood.

He climbed to the top of the hill parallel to me and stopped. The warrior was headed right for me. I put down my musket and pulled out my tomahawk and skinning knife from my belt and watched him approach the tree I was standing behind. As he reached with his right hand to move a tree branch out of his way, I drove my knife into his chest. He dropped to the ground, and I quickly drove my tomahawk into the nape of his neck. He only groaned once. I felt his pulse; he was gone. Yancy was there in a minute. We hid him under some bushes and headed back to where Peter and Leon were.

"We have several choices," Yancy said. "We can wait until they pass, we can make a stand, or we can walk around them."

"What are the best odds?" I asked.

"If we shoot the European and at least two warriors, the rest will run."

We walked the horses farther up the draw. I asked Peter to stay with them, and Leon encouraged him to pet their noses so they would be quiet. Leon, Yancy, and I dropped our packs and took only what we needed. We headed 150 yards down the draw and waited for the band of warriors and the European to approach. Leon couldn't hide his nervousness, so I put my hand on his shoulder to calm him.

"They are coming toward us and are looking for their scout," Yancy said.

They were in and out of the woods bordering the bay. We were elevated on the lower part of the hill looking down into the woods and bay. There was a medium-sized, open area between us and them. Yancy instructed us to wait until they entered the open area. Then we were to fire and quickly reload before they got halfway across it.

The wait was nerve-wracking! I said, "I'll take the European. Leon, you take the warrior to his right, okay?" Leon and Yancy nodded.

They had walked a quarter of the way into the open area when we all fired at the same time. Yancy and I quickly reloaded and fired again. The band disappeared into the woods. We reloaded again. Yancy pointed for us to move uphill. We climbed up fifty yards and hid behind some short trees and shrubs.

Two warriors came at us, and all three of us fired. Yancy motioned for us to move uphill another fifty yards. We quickly reloaded and continued climbing. We were approaching the place where I had killed the first warrior. Looking down the hill past the thick woods, we saw a half dozen warriors running along the edge of the woods and the bay back to where they had come from.

Yancy asked us to go back to where the horses were and find a high position and keep our eyes open. He said he would be back in ten or fifteen minutes. We moved quickly. When we got back to Peter, his eyes told the story. "I heard the musket being fired, but I didn't see any smoke. Is Yancy okay?"

"He'll be back soon. He just wants to make sure they have all left."

Leon and I took positions where we could see anyone approaching. Then we waited. Yancy was gone for quite some time. I knew he was making sure the area was clear, so I told Peter and Leon not to worry. Right after the words were out of my mouth, Yancy walked up the draw, his arms loaded with items. We quickly reached him and helped him carry his load. He had a musket, two backpacks, two bows, and two arrow carriers. He said, "The European and five braves are dead. We have our work cut out for us."

He gave the musket to Peter. A big smile came over his face. We all laughed, mostly from nervous release. We found a quiet place with good soil and plenty of rocks nearby and spent the rest of the day sorting their belongings, burying their bodies along with whatever items we couldn't use or eventually sell, and then properly covering their graves with stones. I said a few words. Then we moved on to find a safe place to camp overnight. It was a quiet evening filled with work and preparation for the next day. We lit no campfire. Before I decided it was time to sleep, I spent some time with the stallion petting him and thanking him for his timely warning.

CHAPTER 18

Lawless

The traffic was picking up. We were running into more Abenaki Indians and, for the first time, some Mohawk Indians and a surprising number of English trappers. Peter talked to the Englishmen and asked them about directions. Grinning from ear to ear, he shared their comments with us. They had all complimented us on our horses.

The St. Lawrence was busy with both canoes and larger boats. We also noticed some ships docked in the harbor. The trip across the river went smoothly. We decided we wouldn't be in a hurry to trade our goods until we knew whom we were dealing with and at what price.

We all had our muskets loaded just in case, and Peter was obvious in his ownership of his new weapon. His musket was longer than our custom-made ones, but I hoped to remedy that issue as soon as we found a musket maker.

It was midday, so there was no hurry to find a place to stay. We walked the streets and located the huge fur-trading post. I asked everyone to wait while I went in and checked it out.

It was very busy with lots of trappers. I walked around and noticed they had the trade values posted on a sign. The trade prices for beaver were 30-40 percent less than in Quebec City. I was sure it was due to the large number of trappers. I stepped back outside and shared my findings. Peter immediately said, "So let's go to Quebec City."

"It's more than one hundred miles to the city," I remarked, and then I thought, *Maybe we can hitch a ride on one of the ships—that is, if they have space.* We headed to the docks, and I asked around. The shipping clerk said there was a small ship leaving the next day. Fortunately, there was space for us, if we were interested, and the price was reasonable. He told us we could load up today and spend the night on the ship, which would save us boarding somewhere. We all agreed to do it.

We found plenty of feed for the horses at a stable near the dock. There wasn't a lot of space in the ship, but the horses settled in quickly. We had plenty of food in our packs, so we made ourselves as comfortable as possible and waited for morning to take our short journey up the river. Having horses on board with us was new for Yancy and Peter. Leon and I enjoyed watching them being barely able to sleep during the night and then staying excited as we sailed up the St. Lawrence River the next day and docked at Quebec City.

We left the ship last just to make sure the horses weren't spooked by anyone or anything. We weren't in any hurry for one of them to fall off the ramp. Back on land, I saw the look of pressure leave Yancy and a smile return to his face as we headed for the trading post and store.

While the associate was checking in the furs, I asked

Yancy what we should pay Peter and Leon. He responded, "Whatever is in your heart."

I didn't want to set them up for disappointment in the future. I figured Leon had made a complete trip to the village and back, plus he was an employee. I didn't like the fact he was an employee. In reality, I liked having partners better. I took him aside and asked, "Would you rather be a partner or an employee?"

He just looked at me; I could see he was thinking. Then he asked, "What's the difference?"

"As an employee you get a monthly stipend, and your pay is regular. As a partner you get a percent of the profits. When things are good, you share; and when things are bad, you share."

"Partnership—I like the sharing part."

The trip was well worth it. When we finished the fur sale and settled up, I handed Leon a fifth of the net profits of the sale in gold and silver. I handed Peter three pieces of silver and told him he was being paid for the full trip now so he could buy what he wanted at the trapper's store. They were both surprised and pleased. I thanked Peter for his suggestion to travel to Quebec City. Yancy thanked me for suggesting the ship. Everyone seemed pleased about something.

On the way to the church, Yancy remarked in a voice loud enough for Peter and Leon to hear, "Great decision on Leon as a partner, and you properly spoiled Peter." To that, we all laughed.

* * *

I looked forward to seeing Fathers Neel and Donne. They were both pulling dead plants out of their garden and appeared excited to see us. They quit working and quickly washed up. They only had a few patients in the mission and invited us to stay. The few left were older Indians who had no other place to stay, Father Neel said, since their fellow villagers had either died or moved away.

The priests almost didn't recognize Peter. He was not only about a foot taller, but he had filled out as well. His hair was shorter, and they had never seen him smile. They each gave him a big handshake and a hug. It was great to see him warm up to them. I could tell the Holy Spirit was growing in his heart. We had cashed out our sale of furs in gold and silver and gave them the four partners' tithes. As usual, they were grateful and thanked us. Leon and Peter watched the transaction and both asked us about it later. It was great to share Henry's Bible lesson that one of the first signs of a Christian's maturity was honoring what Jesus did for us on the cross by tithing. They listened, and I could see understanding in their eyes, or I hoped that's what it was.

We needed to find a place nearby to keep the horses. The priests suggested we tie them up behind the mission and set up temporary wigwams for ourselves—that is, if we wanted to depending on how long we were going to stay. Father Neel said, "No one ever goes back there, and there's a large field of grass for the horses to graze in."

We all left to check it out. The horses quickly became content once their packs were off and they were brushed down. We decided to never leave them alone though. We planned our next few days so each of us could do what he had to do and also share the responsibility of the horses.

The winter sickness had run its course, Father Donne told us, but it wouldn't be too many months before they figured it would start again. He said, "It starts in either late fall or early winter and is over by midsummer. It was a terrible winter of sickness and death. We were both personally blessed not to have gotten sick."

Back inside the mission, I asked Peter if he would like to trade his musket for a custom-made one. His eyes lit up. I had my answer. We ate supper together, which included the nuns and the older guests. Father Neel cooked some fish and we provided some beans and squash. It was nice to eat inside a building again. They were surprised we had traveled to Montreal and then taken a boat to Quebec City. Yancy told them it was cheaper and faster than coming direct, considering the difference in prices for beaver pelts. Everyone shared the high points of the trip, and we talked a little about the attempted robbery.

At breakfast the next morning, we planned our week. Yancy needed two to three days to visit with Chepi and time to catch up on his boat repair investment. I suggested he feel free to take the time and do it. He was pleased but asked me if I was sure it was okay. I encouraged him to do his thing. We would focus on ordering the trade goods and the items on Josh's and Henry's lists, keeping our eyes on the horses, and helping the priests with odd jobs. Fathers Donne and Neel had errands and people to visit most of the week, so we all agreed we wouldn't worry about having meals together until the weekend.

The week passed quickly. We cut wood and filled the church's huge storage bin, finished weeding the vegetable garden, and worked alongside two of the church members pulling weeds and cleaning up bushes around the church. We ordered a new musket for Peter and winter clothes and snowshoes for both Peter and Leon. We rode the horses around the back of the church property just to get comfortable with riding them. We all bought gifts for Josh and Adoette's expected baby. Peter and I bought a doll for Nadie—a surprise gift. Ordering everything else had become routine. Within a few days, we would be heading back to Abenaki Two and then maybe down the river again to Henry's dream lake.

One evening at supper, Leon read a chapter from the book the priests had given me and was applauded for his newly acquired skill. We decided we would talk Nipmuck all the way home this time, hoping we would have it licked by the time we hit the Connecticut River again. Yancy and I weren't betting on it though. Father Donne said he hoped we would continue visiting Quebec City. "Based on the price of furs, I think you can count on it," Yancy replied.

Father Neel gave me a package. "This is for all of you to share."

I opened it. It was a book called, *The Farce of Master Pierre Pathelin* (in English). He went on to tell us it was a play and explained what a play was. He said it was a popular play about four dishonest people and an honest judge. He thought we would like it. He said no one knew the original author, but it was cleverly written in 1465. He bought it for us so we could appreciate what the law was all about and how someday there will be hundreds of laws and judges in New France, and they *will* have a big impact on all kinds of renegades who are never punished today.

Yancy and I looked at each other. I'm sure he was thinking what I was thinking. We knew a few renegades who had recently gotten caught and had paid the price.

Always some new boat on the river.
Courtesy of Jack Mann

CHAPTER 19

Pennacook Indians

Yancy opened up while we were sitting together at breakfast. He mentioned there were problems in the boat repair business and counted them on his fingers as he talked.

1. "There's lots of work, but both craftsmen work limited hours and don't work very fast.
2. Josh's friend, who is also a partner, manages the business and handles the sales, but he hasn't learned how to do much of the work himself.
3. The two craftsmen won't teach the young Indian braves any complex repairs. They just use them as gofers."

He asked me if I had any thoughts on how to make it more profitable. I thought for a moment before saying, "I suggest you and your partners open up your financials to the two tradesmen and three braves and explain to them how they work. You could then offer them a form of partnership for a year. During that year, they would all continue at their same pay and receive a share of the increased profits at the end of each quarter. The sharing concept excites most people I know. If they truly understand the financials, it might motivate them to help improve profits significantly."

Yancy asked, "What share of profit improvement would you offer?"

"Nothing less than 50 percent; and if everyone likes the deal after the first year, maybe the partners would want to make them full partners as we did Leon. That would eliminate their pays and from then on they would just share the net profits."

Yancy said he liked it and asked if I wanted in on the partnership. I laughed and said, "No thanks!"

Yancy's conversation reminded me to write to Grandpa Smith and tell him what had transpired since my previous letter. Late the next evening, I wrote about our successful trapping trip and Leon's amazing skill with the horses and his newly acquired skills of musket shooting and reading and writing French. I told him Yancy and I had made Leon a full partner. I thanked him again for his selection of Leon and the horses and for his love.

Leon asked Yancy how he liked riding bareback. "Is there any other way?" he asked.

"They make saddles for horses and there is a large assortment of types and sizes," Leon happily informed us. It was obvious he was interested in saddles for the business and convinced us to buy one for the resting horse to wear. We found the boot maker and Leon explained to him what he needed. The boot maker told us he had made many saddles when he lived in France. He promised it wouldn't take him long or cost us too much.

We were getting organized and ready to travel again. I knew we wouldn't be back until spring and told that to Fathers Neel and Donne at our last supper together. They agreed it was safer for us to visit in the late spring and summer. They also told us they were starting a school, which they hoped would be up and running by the time we returned. We said our farewells, and I left some extra money for them to invest. Then we packed to head out the next day.

*   *   *

We'd only been out one day when we met three men and a woman headed to Quebec City. They had come from farther up on the St. Lawrence and introduced themselves as Huguenots. They said they had escaped from France with a large group of other Protestants and hoped to move to Montreal and restart their lives. We enjoyed visiting with them and listening to their story. I felt sorry for them, in a way, having to leave their home and loved ones just because they wouldn't renounce their beliefs and join the Catholic Church.

Yancy suggested it might be best if they didn't stop at Montreal because it was part of New France; and as non-Catholics, they wouldn't be able to buy land and build a home. After a rest, we headed our separate ways. It was interesting to see so many people restarting theirs lives in this new land.

We took our old trail to Abenaki One, assuming the family had already moved west. We ran into a few bands of Indians. They were Iroquois and not too friendly, but thank goodness they weren't robbers. As we approached the Abenaki village, we were careful in case they hadn't moved on, but it was barren. We walked through the village. They had stripped it clean. All that was standing were the wigwams, and they were starting to fall apart. It was a sad sight, so we moved on and followed the river to Abenaki Two. The horses were rambunctious. Leon said two of the mares were in heat and wanted the stud to mount them often, which wasn't unusual. I asked him how long it would take to have foals. "It takes a minimum of 320 days."

"You mean maybe next summer?"

"Yes, most likely," he answered.

That would be perfect if we were closer to our permanent home, I thought.

After days and nights passed, we entered Abenaki Two with little fanfare, which was good for a change. Our family joined us and helped us store all our trade goods. I introduced Leon to Henry and Josh as our new full partner; they were delighted. They understood how much he had contributed and how much more profitable he made the business by us not having to hire Indians to tote our goods. We had our own special celebration and handed out gifts, mail, and silver and gold. Everyone was happy. Home cooking is best and Anna and Adoette put on a great welcome home supper. Adoette was starting to show her pregnancy, which made Josh proud. For a while, they were afraid she was going to lose the baby because she had been quite sick early on.

"Henry had kept the medicine man happy while we were gone," Anna said, "although he is ready to move on down the river in spite of the fact it is late fall."

We talked about moving on. I suggested we trade all

our goods first so we could use the horses to tote the heavy personal items like books. We agreed we could carry the furs, but we needed the horses to relocate our heavier personal items. Josh didn't want to move until the baby was born, but Adoette said she was strong enough and could handle it if we decided to move. Henry backed off for the night, but I could feel he had something else on his mind.

The next day, Leon, Yancy, and I were busy doing a lot of trading. Josh and Peter went out to hunt for venison for the village. Henry stopped by to talk. We were rude and spoke French in front of the villagers, but we did it quietly.

"The chief has heard about the diseases from some Abenaki Indians traveling up and down the river, and the threat of a bad winter full of disease is scaring him," Henry said.

"Do you want me to shoot the medicine man or the chief?" I asked.

"Both," he said, with a chuckle.

"I'm a planner and just don't want to put the family in the position of having to leave in midwinter just because a few get sick," Henry said, "and you know they will. It happens every winter. It's the devil in the medicine man that's provoking the chief and the council. We *need* an alternative plan for the winter."

"How about if Yancy and I rent a canoe and head downstream tomorrow to see what we can find? You and Anna cover for us and help Leon with the trading, and we'll find an alternative."

"You are truly my son, Zoel."

*   *   *

We brought some trade goods and three smoked turkeys with us. Yancy and I were on our best behavior. The river was low, so we carefully avoided rocks and stumps. We decided the new village had to be on the river because we were going to buy all the canoes we needed to haul our heavy stuff down the river instead of overland. We moved right along on the river. After two days and nights, we saw a village with fewer than a dozen wigwams. Two warriors welcomed us. We told them we were looking for information.

The village we were looking for was not on this river, they said. It was inland at the junction of two other rivers. The Indians were Pennacook. I asked them about a huge lake. They told us there was one past the river junction farther east on a smaller river. Yancy and I looked at each other and realized we had reached the first part of Henry's vision. I gave each of them a small gift and thanked them. We turned around and headed back up the river. It took us three days of careful, nonstop paddling to get home. The days were long and the nights short, but we safely arrived and quietly entered Abenaki Two.

Henry saw the smiles on our faces as we approached his wigwam. He knew the Lord had shown us the way, and he was anxious to hear about our findings.

CHAPTER 20

Tough Hike

Henry and Anna were overjoyed with our find and were ready to walk to the Pennacook village the next day. Any obstacles to relocating were overcome with thoughtful optimism. It was infectious and to me dangerous, but I didn't want to be a wet blanket. I spoke privately with Leon, Josh, and Yancy about the relocation; they were each concerned for different reasons. We agreed to focus on detailed planning and to be prepared for serious winter weather, sickness of any kind, and robbers.

The mares didn't look as though they were pregnant yet, and Leon couldn't tell. He said they were strong and healthy, and he would pack some hay at the last minute in case we ran into bad weather and they couldn't graze for a day or two. He also convinced everyone to have Adoette and Nadie ride in the new leather saddle to reduce the risk of both of them getting hurt or tired. To make sure they were ready for the trip, he encouraged them to practice by riding around the village on all three mares. They loved it!

Henry let the chief and the council know we were moving on; they were relieved. They asked if they could help in any way. Henry asked them to encourage the villagers to wrap up the trading in two days so the remaining trade goods could be packed away. The whole family worked together to prepare for the trip. Every morning and evening, we reviewed what we had left to do and who was going to do what.

*   *   *

It was late fall. We were finally ready. Josh examined everyone's backpack to make sure it was safe and comfortable. Leon packed the horses' packs personally to make sure they were balanced and not too heavy. Henry's books, my dad's tools, and all the cooking utensils, including pots and pans, were the heaviest items. The horses were more than strong enough to tote them, Leon said.

After eating a light breakfast and saying good-bye to new Christian friends and the rest of the villagers, we headed southeast. The country was new to us. The hills with their hardwood trees and bright, colorful leaves were beautiful. The creeks were many but still shallow from the dry summer. The horses made the trip a pleasure. Each of us carried backpacks of furs and personal bags tied around our waist. Attached to our backpacks were snowshoes for everyone except Nadie. She was riding one of the mares with Adoette. Henry and I figured it would take ten days if all went well and longer if we ran into bad weather.

Four days out and all was well. We killed a few turkeys and decided to leave the deer alone until we felt we were low on smoked venison. We had two hot meals a day—morning and evening—and ate on the run the rest of the day. We gave the horses breaks every two hours and found places where they could rest and graze for fifteen or twenty minutes.

One concern we hadn't talked a lot about was the large number of active black bears we had been seeing. Yancy was the first to notice them and suggested we keep some space, but not too much, between the horses as we traveled. This would give the five of us with muskets room to shoot the bears if they surprised us and attacked.

This time of the year, Josh mentioned, the bears were eating an enormous amount of food getting ready to hibernate through the winter, so we had no idea how many we might run into. He also said we were going to be traveling close to many streams running off the mountains. The mountain berries and the fish in those streams were the bears' primary foods. It was no one's intention to panic the family, but this was a trip loaded with risk. We were focused on reducing that risk by understanding and managing it to the extent we could. We had listened to warriors in the village who had traveled much of the territory, and Josh had penned notes and drawn maps outlining what to avoid and what to look for. We were prepared as well as we could be.

Early on the morning of the fifth day, Yancy was in the lead as usual. We were halfway across a creek that came out of a notch between two steep hills when a charging bear came down the creek and headed straight for Peter. I fired first and then Josh fired. The bear kept coming. Peter faced the charging bear head on and fired. The huge bear dropped in the creek right in front of him. We all cheered Peter's courage and accurate shot.

Yancy and Leon came running to find out what was happening. It took all of us to lift the bear to the soft grass on the side of the creek to examine him closely. There were three bullet holes, two in his upper body and one in the middle of his forehead just above his eyes. Again, we all applauded Peter's shooting skills. Henry said, "That's my boy," and we all laughed. We set up a temporary campsite. Leon found a place for the horses to graze under his and Peter's watchful eyes.

We immediately began the process of gutting the bear and removing the skin, claws, and everything else of value. We decided to stay the night. To celebrate Peter's feat, we ate bear steak for a change. It was a fun night. The weather was cool, but not freezing cold. Anna and I took charge of cleaning the bear skin in the stream. Josh and Yancy quartered it and set up everything to smoke it.

Four days later, we were traveling south below the White Mountains and reached the Pemigewasset River. We had been told this river joined a second river farther east. We stayed above the river to avoid the river debris. We camped for the night. The next morning, we followed the river and noticed some smoke in the distance. As we got closer, it smelled like smoked fish. A mile or so farther, we saw lots of wigwams on a plateau above the river. It was a pretty sight with hardwoods and pines growing behind the wigwams. We noticed a number of people fishing and a few just walking around.

We found a shallow crossing and led the horses into the water. We crossed the river slowly, looking for drop-offs. Some who were fishing along the water's edge pointed to shallower places to walk. They were very friendly and looked closely at the horses. Soon, many villagers gathered and watched us approach the village. The horses had them captivated. A couple of the younger braves looked inquisitively at the smoked bear quarters hanging from the stallion's packs and talked excitedly about the bear meat. As a small crowd gathered, we immediately noticed some of the younger women. They were beautiful!

The chief, with a couple of warriors, introduced himself and asked, "Are you bear hunters?"

"No, not intentionally," I replied. "This one attacked us as we crossed a creek below the mountains; and Peter, this young man standing beside me, killed it. We would never intentionally hunt bear for meat. It's too dangerous and too much work."

They laughed and invited us to join them for a smoke and some hot fish. The chief stopped for a second, looked at us, and asked, "What are those large animals?"

Henry introduced himself and said, "They are horses from across the ocean. They are safe and friendly. If you would like to pet one, come closer." Henry then petted the face of the closest mare; the chief did the same. Then he turned and smiled. That was all it took. The villagers all wanted to have their turn as they led us to the center of their village.

I asked the closest warrior what the name of the other branch of the river was that headed east. He replied, "It's the Winnipesaukee River. It comes from Lake Winnipesaukee."

Henry heard us talking. He turned and smiled and exclaimed, "Can you believe we're here?"

The chief invited us to stay with them. Henry accepted

and asked us to give the chief the bear quarters, which we did. The chief raised one of the quarters in the air and said, "Supper is on our guests." Four of the villagers near him took the quarters and headed for the fire pits. The chief suggested we settle into three wigwams near the tree line and later gather with them for food and fun. He invited Henry to join him in his wigwam, along with what looked like a few of his council members. After Henry removed a small pack from his backpack, I picked up his backpack and headed to our new quarters.

Some village ladies walked with us to the three wigwams and offered to help us unpack and get settled. Three young warriors also joined us. Before they asked lots of friendly questions, the warriors introduced themselves and also offered their services. The village children, we noticed, followed the horses wherever they went. We unloaded the horse packs first and asked the young warriors if there was any grazing grass nearby. Leon, Peter, and the unloaded horses were led behind the wigwams to a small field. After Josh, Yancy, and I organized the three wigwams with everyone's personal packs and the wrapped trade goods, we headed out to help brush down the horses.

Although the Pennacook Indians spoke a different dialect, it was similar to Nipmuck. The beautiful girls I had seen along the shore were nowhere in sight—but not forgotten by Yancy, Leon, Peter, and me. Later at supper, their chief was very friendly and talked a lot about his village and about its preparations for the upcoming winter.

I excused myself and hustled to our wigwam where I collected the bear skin wrapped in buckskin. I returned and set it down next to Henry. The chief went on to tell his villagers we were traders and wanted to trade their beaver and fox furs for items we had brought with us. He also told them, with the council's approval, he had invited us to stay the winter. Everyone seemed to be pleased. Henry stood up and thanked him and the council and handed the chief the wrapped gift. "This is a gift of thanks for the offer to let us stay with you for the winter."

Everyone cheered when the chief removed the bear skin from its wrapping and held it up for all to see. We had found an advocate and a new home. Henry's vision was unfolding. Before we all headed to our beds, we gathered in Henry's wigwam, held hands in a circle, and Henry prayed, "Thank you, Lord, for your amazing grace, mercy, love, protection, and our new winter home. Please use us as conduits of your Holy Spirit so some of the villagers will get to know you. Amen."

CHAPTER 21

Mating

The weeks that followed were like the two books given to us by Fathers Neel and Donne. Life in the village seemed surreal. The people, we were told, are very healthy most of the time, including wintertime. Their problem was having too many ladies and too few warriors. The council was studying the problem and thought it might be because of the village's primary reliance on fish and vegetables for food, but no one knew for sure.

Kiddingly, I asked the family at supper after we'd been there awhile if I could officially tell the council that four of their new guests were intimidated by the number and beauty of the unmarried women. It wasn't that they were just beautiful, but they were also excellent cooks and worked hard with the other women of the village cleaning and smoking the fish the warriors had hooked or speared while canoeing or had caught in the river with their nets.

Henry responded to my question by saying, "We catch your meaning, but we don't think it would be wise for you to share your feelings unless *you* are ready to get married." That comment made everyone laugh.

There was lots of competition for the available village warriors. Some said it was good for the village, but I couldn't see how or why. I decided to keep my eyes open and not focus on any particular single lady for more than a few seconds. With that strategy, I hoped to avoid any misinterpretation of my intentions, but it wasn't easy.

It was nice just to sit alone on the bank of the river and watch eagles swoop down and grab fish and then head to a tall tree where sometimes a partner was waiting. The Pemigewasset and the Winnipesaukee Rivers joined and created the new and much larger river called the Merrimack. Canoeing the Merrimack reminded me of the Connecticut River as it weaved around rolling hills and headed south to some magic new land. I wondered if someday my children would canoe down the river and discover where it dumped its crystal clear water.

As days and then weeks passed, we worked side by side with the other villagers gathering wood and cleaning and smoking the fish and deer we killed. We had stored the trade goods, family tools, and smoked meats in a wigwam between Henry's and Josh's wigwams. Josh also kept all the packs and many of our personal items wrapped and stored in his wigwam. The family was security conscious and didn't want to create an easy opportunity for someone to steal, mainly because we wanted to keep the peace and stay the winter.

One day, the chief asked Henry to invite Leon, Yancy, Peter, and me to his wigwam for supper. Henry said he thought it might be fun and suggested we accommodate him. After all, we were the chief's guests.

The chief's family served a mighty tasty supper. While we were eating, the chief said he had something he wanted to tell us.

"We are delighted with the four of you and want you to consider joining our village. We have too many unmarried daughters and offer you your choice as long as they also choose you. We will build each of you a new wigwam for your family and also give you a new canoe. We believe you will come to love and think of our village as your home and the villagers as your family."

This was a serious offer. We were dumbfounded. The four of us just looked at each other. I finally recovered and looked directly at the chief and asked, "May I say something before anyone else answers?"

"Please do, Zoel."

"We respect your offer. I have talked to each man here, and we all agree your ladies are beautiful and would make wonderful wives."

"Thank you."

I continued, "We are on a mission and are committed to finish that mission before we dedicate ourselves to any other responsibility like a wife, a family, or a village. We need to continue to help Henry set up a mission to serve the sick and abandoned Indians who live in this area. If you haven't talked to Henry about his vision, I hope you will soon. We believe in what he is striving to accomplish, and our focus needs to be on helping him and nothing else."

"So, in a way you're saying he is your chief?"

"Yes, in many ways he is."

"Do you all feel the same way?" The others nodded their heads and said yes. "Is there any way I can bribe one of you?" he asked kiddingly.

It was an excellent supper. We gained respect for the chief and what he was trying to do, but we weren't ready for marriage. We all thanked him for his time and the great food and headed back to our wigwams and to the horses Josh was watching for us. On the way, we cracked jokes about whether we did the right thing and, of course, which girl we each might have had on our mind.

Henry came out and visited the horses after dark and wanted to chat. I was sure he had already talked to Peter about the meeting with the chief. "How did it go?" he asked. I shared our conversation and my thoughts.

"He's just trying to do his job, Zoel." I agreed. "Do you think the four of you will come back after the mission is built and select a wife?"

"It depends on how many will respond to God's calling through the Holy Spirit and accept Jesus as their Savior, Henry."

"Maybe we need to pray about that with the rest of the family," he said before leaving and bidding me a good night.

He is a wise father and a good leader, I thought to myself after he left.

*   *   *

The temporary wigwams worked great as mini homes to live in while we took care of the horses. It was more fun for me to sleep and quarter near the horses than it was to be in the center of the village for many reasons, but most of all for the privacy.

Peter moved back in with Henry and Anna—at their request—although he wasn't excited about it. Having left the nest, I found it had been fun to go back for a little while, but I sincerely loved my freedom and privacy. Yancy and Leon were in the same boat as I. That was good.

The three of us had a lot in common; and as time passed, we shared more. Yancy wanted out of his partnership in the boat repair business and said he knew Josh did also. He and Josh had good intentions and hoped the business was successful, but they no longer had any interest in living in or near any busy community like Quebec City. They had in the back of their minds to take one more trip there to sell furs and, at the same time, to sell their interest in the business to Josh's friend from France. Yancy said they had learned they were going to have to personally manage full-time whatever business they invested in.

Leon and I were more comfortable living near cities, we thought, but didn't like the risk of catching any serious disease. We all talked about venereal disease, and the only way to totally avoid it was abstinence. Yancy was older and said there were so many untainted, beautiful women to marry that only a fool would play around and destroy his future health and the future health of his eventual wife.

Leon decided just after the first snowfall that at least two of the mares were pregnant. He also said the other mare was now in heat, and we might have a busy summer and fall next year. It was all good news to me. The more horses the merrier.

The deeper the snow got, the more space we gave the horses to forage for food. They had no problem moving snow aside and eating the grass below it. They seemed to sense where the best grass was and would stop, dig for a few seconds, and then eat. Most of the village children had lost interest in them, which made our world much simpler and safer.

We all noticed the village chief called Henry "Priest." It started the first day we arrived and crossed the river. It appeared the chief didn't hear Henry say his first name when he introduced himself. Now it was locked in. He was Priest again just like he had been called on the ship during our voyage from France to New France. As days passed, the rest of the villagers also called him Priest. He didn't care as long as the chief and the council let him hold Bible classes. At Anna's suggestion, he held two separate classes: one for men and one for women. More people attended than ever before. Henry was amazed! He described the classes as completely different and credited Anna with making them much more vibrant and fun for the attendees as well as much easier for him. "This," he said, "is a prime example of the right woman making a real difference in a man's vocation."

CHAPTER 22

Winter Home

Winter moved in on us slowly. The village was well stocked with smoked fish and venison; nevertheless, we never stopped hunting and fishing. The crops had done well, and the gardens had been cleaned up for weeks. Most families were stocked up with a good supply of squash and beans as well as corn in many forms. The women of the village had focused on making deerskin winter clothes. At an outdoor luncheon on one of those Indian summer days, the chief's new bear coat was put on display for everyone to admire and touch.

Henry's Bible classes became weekly social events that many wouldn't think of missing. The classes began in midmorning and sometimes included lunch. At first, the ladies classes included a light lunch; then the menu expanded. The men decided to have lunch every other meeting. They served themselves venison steak and beans and Henry's turkey broth as a hot drink. Even the chief began attending the men's classes.

I couldn't remember a more welcoming village or a more open community. Even the medicine man was open to learning and listening about Jesus. We knew it was driven by the Holy Spirit and was an answer to prayer. We were thankful.

The river grew cold, but ice had a hard time forming on the fast-moving water. Thin ice had formed in some of the coves, but where the rivers joined there was little hope for ice. Our snowshoes were a hit, and the canoe builders took orders and made snowshoes that were functional, but they were not as good as the ones we had bought in Quebec City.

The horses' coats thickened and were like European sheep's wool. They looked like different animals, but they had no problem feeding themselves. They would forage for grass in a limited area on our end of the village and then always come in close to our temporary wigwams before dark for more water. We tied them up at night—just in case. One of us checked on them periodically twenty-four hours a day. The two pregnant mares were slowly getting wider, but their attitudes hadn't changed.

*   *   *

One morning just after dawn, I heard all kinds of screaming and commotion in the village. Yancy, Leon, and I grabbed our muskets and headed toward the sound. We had only gotten ten steps out of our wigwam when we heard a musket go off and saw the smoke. We ran toward it. Peter was leaning over a dead black bear. Two warriors had been attacked by the bear and were being helped by Anna, Henry, and the medicine man.

The bear, we learned, had been searching for food in the village. The warriors tried to kill it before it ripped into the storage wigwam between Henry's and Josh's. One of the warriors said Peter came running out of Henry's wigwam. The bear saw him, stood up, growled, and headed for him. Peter shot him in the head, and the bear dropped dead at his feet. The three of us rolled the bear over. Peter's bullet had hit it in the forehead just above its eyes.

Henry looked over at me while he was cleaning one of the warrior's cuts and asked, "What do you think of my body guard?"

I laughed. All I could say was that "his presence in your wigwam was no accident, Henry." He knew what I meant and nodded his head in agreement.

One warrior's cut healed quickly. The other warrior had multiple wounds and was slowly healing. The villagers used the attack as an opportunity to celebrate by serving bear meat to everyone at one of those warm midday luncheons. The chief presented Peter with his own bear coat, which he said he couldn't accept. He asked the chief to give it to the warrior who was still suffering from his injuries. The chief was pleased to do that. The legend of Peter's quick response to the crisis, courage in the face of danger, accuracy with a musket, and his giving heart was repeated over and over all winter long. It amazed me how far Peter had come in such a short time. *This young Englishman has it all.*

* * *

As the weather got worse, we had lots of time to talk and plan for spring and the next year. Henry was not as eager to move to Lake Winnipesaukee as he had been just a month ago. Anna and Nadie had quickly made good friends there. Peter, comfortable and not eager to move on, had involved himself in the men's Bible study group. His Nipmuck was improving dramatically, as was Leon's. I remember Henry saying, "To learn a language is to live it." He was right.

Once Josh and Adoette's baby was born, he and Yancy planned to travel to Quebec City to settle their affairs. We had trapped 75 percent of the furs in storage and the other 25 percent were mostly fox and lynx skins. Some of the warriors had learned to trap beaver. But during the winter, the beavers seldom came out of their huts on the frozen water. This meant the trip wasn't going to be very profitable unless we all trapped beaver in the early spring.

Leon and I were focused on the four horses and looking forward to the birth of the foals the following year. Leon suggested we not use the two pregnant mares to haul anything—that is, if we wanted to maximize our chances of having healthy foals. We all agreed. I mentioned to everyone that the two foals, if sold, could produce more gold and silver than we could make on one trip of furs to Quebec City. I hoped this would refocus Josh's and Yancy's priorities.

I asked them both how much they would lose if they just walked away from their investment in Quebec City. When they told me, I realized it was nothing compared to what I had in savings—maybe 10 percent. If they were willing to walk away, I suggested, I would make them whole.

Astonished, they both asked, "Why would you do that?"

"The trip you both will take *may* break even and, as you know, it's very dangerous for many reasons. Your safety and eliminating the risk is more important to me than the money it would cost me. To me, this will boil down to an issue of pride. Can you let me help you walk away? I can't forget how much you two have done for me. So, *please* let me help you do this! You don't have to answer now. Pray about it first, and then we'll talk, okay?"

Henry came to me the next morning and gave me his you-are-my-good-son smile. "Adoette, Anna, and I thank you for what you are doing."

"You're all very welcome. Not to change the subject, but can we talk about your plans for the spring?"

He outlined his desire to visit the village on Lake Winnipesaukee because he was getting closer to where he saw the permanent home for the mission. Because the two horses couldn't carry all the goods, I suggested he consider making his first trip in canoes. He wasn't excited about using them, but he said he'd think about it.

"Have you mentioned this to anyone else yet?" he asked.

"No, and I won't until you're ready."

For many reasons, the winter was terrible; for many other reasons, the winter was wonderful. Many new friendships were established, and many villagers came to know the Lord through Henry's Bible classes. Compared to any other village or town we had stayed or lived in, very few people were sick. I wondered if it was because of the high percentage of fish everyone ate in this village as compared to other villages. It was also a wonderful planning time. We talked in alternatives and listened to everyone's opinion. No one was in a hurry. There was no place to go.

We laid a second cover of deerskins over the wigwams

to make them warmer and moved our small fires inside. We were still cold no matter how much we wore or how much wood we burned. It was the first time I envied the fur coats of animals. The horses—their winter coats about four inches thick—appeared to be comfortable as long as they were out of the wind. I missed the sun. I missed its penetrating warmth and beautiful brightness. The grey, wintry days and long, dark, bitter cold nights on the river just went on and on.

CHAPTER 23

Yancy's Home

The two mares were getting bigger, but they still didn't look uncomfortable. Most people wouldn't have noticed. But because I was with them every day, I could feel as well as see their bodies change. Their temperaments were also starting to change. They were a little irritable but only when the stallion wasn't around. "The other mare wasn't pregnant," Leon said, "at least not yet."

The weather was improving, and the snow was mostly gone. We could, however, still see lots of it on the White Mountains. It was beautiful! The rivers were filling up as well as warming up—a little. The warriors, in full force, were back fishing on the river, and the villagers were kept busy smoking their catch. Everyone was enjoying the beginning of spring. And Adoette was just about ready to give birth.

During those dreary, cold winter days, most of the villagers had stayed in their wigwams; therefore, we didn't see many of the beautiful ladies very often. Now that the weather was warming, they were like new leaves on the trees. They were everywhere. Some of them accompanied their younger brothers and sisters when they came to pet the horses. They were friendly and always had questions. Yancy seemed to especially enjoy the visits of one particular lady. She responded to his friendliness by visiting more often. It was the first time I had seen Yancy seriously interested in any eligible woman. After one particular visit, Yancy checked with Anna to see if she attended the Bible study sessions. The answer was "yes, and she has committed her heart to Jesus." From then on, it was only a matter of weeks before they announced their engagement. They were married in the spring on a warm Saturday morning and moved in with Josh and Adoette.

Yancy's wife's name was Halona (of happy fortune). The chief honored his commitment to build a wigwam and a canoe for the new couple. Everybody got involved in both projects. Leon helped on the wigwam, and I helped building the canoe. When the wigwam and canoe were finished, the chief made a special presentation welcoming Yancy to the village as a permanent brother and asked him to join the leadership council. From that point on, we all knew Yancy would never leave. He was a natural leader. The village people loved him and his caring nature as well as the fact he never forgot a name. I could see him as a chief someday—that is, if he wanted to be.

*   *   *

I suggested to Yancy and Josh that we take a ride up the Winnipesaukee River in Yancy's new canoe. It was a beautiful canoe and a beautiful day. Paddling, we could feel the warm sun and the cold splashes of river water. We stopped along the shoreline and walked a little way up the north bank. While we sat there overlooking the river and the distant village, I asked them, "Have you thought about my offer to make you whole on your investments?"

"Yes," they both answered, "but we feel bad about taking your money."

"You underestimate the value of what each of you has done for me. I would be honored if you would accept it." They *finally* agreed!

Then they asked me what my plans were. I shared, "If you two will escort Henry to his new village after the baby's birth, it will free me up to travel with Leon to Quebec City to sell our furs—that is, assuming we can continue collecting what we need to make the trip profitable. I'll be happy to deliver letters to your partner releasing him of any obligation to repay your investments. If there is anything else I can do for either of you while I'm there, just let me know."

They were both pleased and thanked me again. For the first time in both of their lives, they said, they had lost interest in traveling far away from home. I told them I understood why.

When we returned to the village, they put together a plan to get more warriors involved in trapping beaver. They did it by promising better deals on the trade goods we still had in inventory. I met with Henry and Peter; they agreed it would be smarter to use canoes to travel to the new village on Lake Winnipesaukee, plus the canoes would give them the ability to tour the lake and eventually witness to other bands of Indians. Henry met with the chief and asked him if he would help organize a trade of some of our goods for new canoes. The chief thought it was a great idea. Within a month, Henry had traded for two new canoes; and Josh, Yancy, and their warrior friends had finished trapping enough beaver to make the trip to Quebec City very profitable.

Henry and I were headed separate ways again. We both knew the Lord was with us, and Leon's and my trip would continue to help finance the spreading of the Gospel to Indians living on Lake Winnipesaukee.

Josh and Adoette's baby, Yvonne Mary, named after Josh's mother, was born big and healthy. We all celebrated. To no one's surprise, Adoette was on her feet the next day doing her daily chores. *She is one strong and healthy woman,* I thought to myself.

Josh and Yancy had developed friendships with many newly married couples in the village. Two of the couples, who loved the horses, had agreed to watch over the two pregnant mares while Leon and I were gone. We had the stallion and the other mare packed and prepared to make the trip to Quebec City. We wore our old, comfortable backpacks and carried our weapons, including our muskets. Just before leaving, Henry said he would be headed out within weeks of our leaving. We agreed to pray daily for each other and for the rest of the family. Nadie, my growing and constantly talking little sister, gave me a big hug and made me feel special with a small bracelet she had made for me with Anna's help, of course. It reminded me of the bracelet Sooleawa had made for me not so long ago. Now ready to leave, we said farewell to everyone.

*   *   *

Leon and I were back on the trail. It felt refreshing to be alone again in the wilderness near the White Mountains. It was almost like being in another world. The snow was still there, but it was higher up the mountains. The melting snow filled the creeks and created beautiful sounds when we stopped to listen. The birds provided never-ending music, and the cool breezes warned us not to dress too lightly.

With spring came the presence of many black bears, which were now out of hibernation and hungry. We saw them fishing in the creeks and rivers and kept our distance. With just the two of us and the bulk of the weight being carried by the two horses, we made good time. With the clear, dry nights, we skipped making temporary wigwams and didn't stop to shoot anything until we were low on smoked turkey and venison.

We met no one on the trip until the day we sighted the St. Lawrence River in the distance. A small band of Iroquois warriors appeared to be out hunting. They had no war paint on and were *almost* friendly. They took long looks at our horses and our muskets and passed at a distance.

Leon asked, "Why can't they be friendly?"

"I have no idea, but I'm keeping my musket in a ready position just in case."

The stallion was my companion on the entire trip. I didn't have to do anything but walk. He kept pace with me. The rope in my hand was just an emergency line. I could hear him breathing; I was sure he could hear me doing the same, especially on the hills. It was wonderful owning horses, and I couldn't imagine living without them now.

The river and the city were changing. The docks were expanding on the south side of the river, and the port was expanding on the north side. The city was warming up from an excessively cold winter, and all shared how pleased they were with the arrival of spring. The boat ride went fine. Once in the city, we headed for the trading post and completed our fur sale. We then headed to Josh and Yancy's boat repair business and dropped off the letters to the young French owner. We didn't stay for any conversation but instead headed to the church to see our two friends again.

The church was under construction. The new walls were enormous, and the new tower with its beautiful roof was an impressive sight. We walked to the back of the church where we had kept the horses the last time. We noticed some children gathered under a tree with Father Donne. He appeared to be reading from the book he was holding. He saw us, closed his book, and waved as we approached. "As you can see, we have started the school."

After some robust handshakes, he introduced us to the children, and we introduced the horses to them. The children loved the horses, and the horses loved the attention and stood still while the children talked to them and petted their faces and necks.

After the horses had been brushed down and made comfortable, we set up a large temporary wigwam. Then we cleaned up and joined our two friends for dinner. We exchanged letters, local gossip, and family news. That took most of the evening. Leon and I were both excited by the joy we could see in Fathers Neel and Donne as they shared what the Lord had done for them since our last visit.

Good to be back on the mountain trail again.
Courtesy of Jack Mann

CHAPTER 24

The Sickness

Josh and Yancy's partner stopped by the church while I was at the trapper's store ordering our items. He left envelopes for Josh and Yancy. When I got back, Father Neel said the young man wanted to make sure Josh and Yancy received the envelopes. He said he had assured him they would be delivered.

I made a visit to Yancy's friend Chepi, the lady who worked at the dressmaker's shop and cared for the young, orphaned girls. At Yancy's request, I left her a large gift of money to help with expenses. Two of the six girls, she said, had been placed in nice homes, and she was optimistic that within the next six months the other girls would also be placed. She mentioned she was getting married soon and wanted me to let Yancy know that and that she wouldn't need any more financial help from him. She said she was very, very appreciative of his help and wanted me to thank him for his generous gifts. I told her I would share the information with him and wished her well.

We ordered a limited number of trade goods, considering we had only two horses. Then we stopped by the musket

159

maker's shop and asked if he would check out and clean our weapons. He did it while we waited. He also brought us up to date on some new pistols that would be available within a few months. We both told him we were interested and would stop by the next time we were in town.

The priests were pleased to receive our tithes. I asked about the new building construction. Father Neel shared that one of their newest members was very rich. He thought the church needed upgrading and was funding the improvements. I asked if he also helped with the poor. Father Donne said he was only into upgrading the church building, which was why they were so thankful for *our* gifts. I knew in my heart my probing question was out of line and quickly apologized for it.

Father Neel talked about England and France. They were about to go to war over many different things, including beaver furs and dried cod. He said we should keep our eyes open for English sympathizers. I responded by telling them, "The price we received for our furs was the best price we had ever been paid, and the trade associate at the trading post said the fear of a war was pushing up the prices."

I gave them additional money to help with the sick and the poor and a letter to be mailed to my grandfather in which I shared much of what had happened since my previous letter to him. Father Donne gave me some mail and a package for Henry. It was heavy and felt like a large book. Father Donne asked me to treat it carefully and to make sure it didn't get wet, so I put it in the top of my backpack. It was time to leave; we said our good-byes.

*   *   *

Summer was approaching, and we were itching to hit the trail. Ready to head out, we picked up our supplies and trade goods at the trapper's store. We both tried to make sure we had everything, including the gifts for Nadie and for Josh's new baby, which I had almost forgotten to buy. Once everything was paid for and packed away, we proceeded to the docks to take a boat across the river.

It was still early in the day, and we weren't in any hurry. The boats were busy, so we waited and watched. There were a lot of Europeans heading both ways across the river. Some were English, some were Dutch, and very few were French. It was unusual to hear the different languages being spoken. In the past, French and Nipmuck were the only languages we would hear. If war came, Leon and I agreed that the Pennacook village on the Merrimack River would be a safer place to be than in or near Quebec City.

We finally got a ride across the river and headed home the way we had come. We ran into a few travelers; but the farther away we got from Quebec City, the fewer people we saw. Leon wanted to talk about a few things he had on his mind. So the first night we stopped a little earlier than usual and prepared a good, hot supper. He had been thinking about his future and wondered what my plans were after we got Henry set up in his new mission on the lake. I told him I had some ideas but wanted to hear what he was thinking about first.

He recalled my comment to the family that selling the two foals after they were born would bring in more money than one fur-trading trip. I told him I recalled saying it. He went on and asked, "How do you feel about breeding and selling horses as well as trapping and fur trading?"

"I think it's an interesting idea, but who would buy the horses?"

"Farmers, trappers, and fur traders like us would buy them. Plus, many people in big cities could use them to haul items like those needed to upgrade a church. If they had horses and carts, it would make their construction work easier and less expensive."

"Where would we live if we were fully involved in the business?"

"I think we could live anywhere as long as we were willing to travel to cities to sell our foals just as we travel to sell our furs now."

"Would we need more than one stallion?"

"No, not initially as long as we're able to trade or sell each stud and filly produced by our stallion. If we traded our stallion's filly each time for another filly not in his breading line, we should be able to maintain a very healthy and large breeding line of horses. And, of course, regular exercise is important to keep the horses healthy."

"I must tell you, Leon, I like getting two for one—trading furs and horses on the same trip. It either means twice as much profit or half as many trips or maybe both. What would you do next to grow the business?"

"On our next trip, I would trade the mare that is with us today—if she doesn't produce by winter—for another filly, and I would trade the two foals when they are born for breeding mares or even a second stallion. I would also buy a second saddle so you and I could ride each of the horses frequently."

"I like your plan, Leon. Let's talk more about it as we

travel and then share it with the family when we get home, okay?"

"Sure, and thanks for listening, Zoel. I'm glad you like my idea."

The rest of the trip went well, and we made sure we didn't spook the number of black bears and the two moose we saw. We shot a number of turkeys and smoked what we didn't eat. The horses grazed off and on all day and into the late evenings of our long summer days. We saw two bands of Indians, but they weren't headed anywhere near us. It was great traveling in the high hills because we could see what was coming and going from a long way off. We arrived at the Pemigewasset River's edge at midday. Farther down, we noticed the river was full of canoes with warriors fishing. As we crossed it, everyone waved to us; it was good to be welcomed home.

*   *   *

We were surprised everyone was still there. We expected Henry and Peter—at a minimum—to be at the village on Lake Winnipesaukee. All went out of their way to welcome us and helped us unpack both horses. We delivered everyone's envelopes, packages, gifts, and share of the profits. Everyone was smiling. The afternoon was filled with thanks and lots of questions. By the time supper was finished, we had nothing left to tell them.

It was their turn to bring us up to date. Henry said he was disappointed and, at the same time, elated about the trip he, Yancy, Josh, and Peter had taken up the Winnipesaukee River. The village there was experiencing a sickness. Therefore, the warriors they had met at the edge of the village recommended they not enter it at that time. The Winnepisseogee Indian village was large. It was on the north side of the lake and many of the villagers were in the process of moving to the east side away from the main village to avoid whatever was killing the old and the young.

As a result, they decided they wouldn't enter the village and instead headed back down the west side of the lake past the exit of the Winnipesaukee River, which they had come though the day before. There, they found a large bay and a smaller back bay. Henry recognized his mission site the moment he saw it.

Henry said his goals right now were to continue with his weekly Bible study classes *and* to make plans to build a mission in the back bay as soon as reasonably possible. I was delighted for him and the family and told him so with a big hug. I congratulated everyone else. We all realized this finding was a big deal. It was an answer to many months and years of praying.

Anna said they had been talking about opening the mission to those who were sick on the lake, which would mean they would have to isolate themselves until the sickness passed to keep the Pennacook village from being exposed. Yancy shared that everyone in the village knew what Henry and Anna were intending to do. And as long as they didn't expose the village to the sickness, the villagers were comfortable.

"Has anyone even started to put a plan together yet, Henry?"

"No, Zoel, we were waiting for you." That comment caused laughter from everyone. I obviously had a new job to do.

Leon and I kept our thoughts about our horse-breeding business to ourselves. We all wanted the mission built and established before winter, which meant we had to plan out every step and share it with the chief and the council to keep them and the entire village safe and comfortable with what we intended to do.

I suggested we treat the Back Bay site as two missions: one part for those who were seriously ill and a separate section for those who were not so ill. The center of the seriously ill section would include a large wooden building. We should also build fire pits and wigwams near the building to support the isolation of the seriously ill.

Separate from that area, I suggested we build many wigwams with their own fire pits. It was critical that all the buildings be completed without any contact with those on the lake who had any symptoms of the sickness. Everyone in the family, the chief, and the village council members liked the plan and agreed to help.

Three weeks later, twenty-five canoes loaded with our entire family, warriors, axes, hammers, nails, hundreds of deerskins, all of Henry's, Anna's, Peter's, and Nadie's personal items, and enough food to feed the army of helpers for at least two weeks headed up the Winnipesaukee River to build a mission in Back Bay on Lake Winnipesaukee. I found it profound that the Lord had led Smith and Priest to this particular lake, which name means "smile of the Great Spirit."

Afterword

The Connecticut River Valley had provided the family with a safe harbor during many cold winter days and nights. Abenaki One and Two had been wonderful villages to call home, and Henry's Bible teachings, through the power of the Holy Spirit, had won souls and yielded fruit for God's kingdom. Having found the perfect spot for the mission Henry had envisioned, Back Bay Mission is built on the huge lake south of the snow-capped White Mountains and serves the abandoned and sick Indians both medically and spiritually.

Zoel and his new partner, Leon Durand, continue to support the Quebec City Mission and the Back Bay Mission. Horses materially change their business and personal lives. Their adventures continue in the upcoming publication of *Anna's Courage*. Look for it at CrossBooks.com.

References and Notes

- The Québec Series, <u>Quebec, the First Nations and European Explorations</u>. Wikipedia, the free encyclopedia at http://en.wikipedia.org/wiki/Quebec.

  - The name Quebec, where the St. Lawrence River narrows to a tree-lined gap, comes from the Algonquin word *kébec* meaning "where the river narrows."
  - The First Nations and European explorers in Quebec found Algonquin, Iroquois, and Inuit Indians there.
  - Many lived nomadic lives hunting, gathering, and fishing in the Canadian Shield and the Appalachian Mountains.
  - Others lived more settled lives planting squash and maize in the St. Lawrence River Valley.
  - James Cartier in 1534 planted a cross and claimed the land for the King of France.
  - Samuel de Champlain, as part of an expedition

from France, sailed into the St. Lawrence River and returned in 1608 to found Quebec City.

- With the eventual military alliance between the Algonquin and Heron nations, France established a permanent fur-trading outpost in what was then called New France.
- From Quebec, voyagers and Catholic missionaries used river canoes to explore the North American continent.
- It wasn't long before King Louis XIII forbade anyone other than Roman Catholics from settling in New France. He also encouraged immigration from the motherland to New France.

- Introduction, <u>Quebec City</u>. Wikipedia, the free encyclopedia at http://en.wikipedia.org/wiki/Quebec_City.

- Samuel de Champlain, a French explorer and diplomat, founded the city on July 3, 1608.
- Samuel served as its administrator until his death.
- St. Lawrence Iroquoians had lived where the city was founded, but there was no trace of them in 1608.
- By 1665 there were 550 people and 70 houses in the city.
- One-quarter of the people were from religious orders, including priests, Jesuits, Ursulines nuns, and the order running the local hospital, Hotel-Dieu.

- Between 1608-1627 and 1632-1723, it was the capital of New France.
- It is on the north bank of the St. Lawrence River near its meeting with the St. Charles River.
- The region is low lying, flat, and good for farming.

- Chapter 1, <u>Wigwam</u>. Wikipedia, the free encyclopedia at http://en.wikipedia.org/wiki/Wigwam.

  - The male in the family usually built the frame of the wigwam.
  - It was permanent and would hold up to all weather conditions.
  - The wigwams were rounded or conical structures.
  - They were ten to sixteen feet in diameter.
  - The frame was made from cut and bent green tree saplings. The tall saplings were used in the middle, and the shorter ones were used on the outside of the circle. Additional saplings were wrapped around the wigwam.
  - The sides and roof were covered with grass, brush, mats, reeds, hide, and/or cloth.

- Chapter 1, <u>Vermont Indian Tribes and Languages</u>. Found at http://www.native-languages.org/vermont.htm.

- The Abenaki Indians lived in the upper half of Vermont bordering the Connecticut River.
- The Pennacook Indians lived in southeastern Vermont bordering the Connecticut River.
- They spoke Abenaki-Penobscot, an Algonquian language still spoken today.
- Eastern Abenaki or Penobscot was another dialect spoken in Maine.
- The Abenaki and Pennacook Indians were adversaries of the Iroquois Indians.
- During the 1500s-1600s, 75 percent of the native New England Indians died from diseases contracted from the Europeans.
- When many died, the survivors merged with other tribes, and their identities became blurred.

- Chapter 1 and referred to in many other chapters, <u>Canoe</u>. Wikipedia, the free encyclopedia at http://en.wikipedia.org/wiki/Canoe.

  - The parts of a canoe include the bow, stern, and hull.
  - Charcoal and fats were mixed into the resin of tar.
  - The white cedar frame was tied together with tree roots.
  - Pine pitch was used to waterproof it.
  - Birch bark was used to cover the frame.

- Chapter 1, <u>Native American Names and Meanings Pg1</u>. Found at http://www.snowwowl.com/swolfNAnamesand-meanings.html.

  - The first groups of Algonquin Indians that the French encountered were the Kichesipirini who, because their village was on an island in the Ottawa River, were called *La Nation de I'Ilse*.
  - Among themselves, the Algonquin Indians differentiated between bands: those that remained in the upper Ottawa Valley year-round and those that moved to the St. Lawrence River during the summer – the northerners being called *Nopiming daje Inini* (inlanders).

- Algonquin names and their meanings:

- Female:

  - Adoette   (big tree)
  - Halona   (of happy fortune)
  - Nadie   (wise)
  - Sooleawa   (silver)
  - Chepi   (fairy)
  - Anna   (mother)

- Male:

  - Etu   (sun)
  - Ezhno   (solitary)

- Chapter 2, <u>Beaver</u>. Wikipedia, the free encyclopedia at http://en.wikipedia.org/wiki/beaver.

  - Beavers have castor sacs that they use to mark their territories. This secretion includes salicin, which they get from eating the bark of willow trees. It was used as a painkiller as aspirin is today. It was also used to raise the heart output and blood pressure.
  - Beaver testicles were also used for the same above-stated purposes.
  - Both items were also used as anti-inflammatory medicines and to reduce fevers.
  - Beaver pelts were shipped and used to make felt hats in Europe. Europeans had killed off all their beaver. It is estimated that at one time there were as many as 90 million beavers in North America. It is also estimated that there are between 15 and 30 million today.

- Chapter 2 and referred to in other chapters, <u>Canadian Horse History</u>. Found at http://www. eidnet.org/local/cdnhorse/history.htm.

  - In 1665 Louis XIV sent two stallions and twenty mares from the royal stables to the colony in New France.
  - In 1667 and 1670 additional horses were sent to the colonies and helped establish sufficient horses to support the community's needs.

- The horses originally came from Normandy and Brittany, places known for having excellent, if small, horses.
- The horses had strong constitutions and survived with little help when they were not in use.
- The tails on the horses were usually docked, which meant it was hard for them to keep flies away from their body parts during the hot summers.

- Chapters 2 and 3, <u>Connecticut River Valley</u>. Wikipedia, the free encyclopedia at http: // en.wikipedia.org/wiki/Connecticut_River.

  - The Connecticut River is the largest river in New England.
  - It flows south from the Connecticut Lakes in northern New Hampshire along the border between Vermont and New Hampshire.
  - It is 407 miles long and drains into Long Island Sound.

- Chapter 3, <u>Musket</u>. Wikipedia, the free encyclopedia at http://en.wikipedia.org/wiki/Musket.

  - The need to defeat armor led to the development of the musket.
  - Between the years 1550-1650, the musket continued to penetrate 2 mm thick armor. A stand was used to hold up the heavy weapon.

- Between the years 1630-1660, the weapon was shortened from four feet to three feet and the rest was given up.

- Chapter 10, <u>Vinegar</u>. Wikipedia, the free encyclopedia at http://en.wikipedia.org/wiki/Vinegar.

  - Vinegar's key ingredient is acetic acid (ethanoic acid).
  - Its fermentation sources include wine, cider, beer, and fruit juices.
  - It has been used since ancient times.
  - The word comes from the French word *vinaigre* (sour wine).
  - White vinegar is used on sunburns to cool the skin.
  - White vinegar is used for cleaning hard surfaces.
  - Taken with food, it increases fullness and can help one lose weight.
  - It is used as a natural deodorant to kill bacteria.
  - It is used as a hair conditioner and also untangles hair. Rinsing eliminates the smell when the hair dries.
  - Vinegar is used as an herbicide because it is not absorbed by the roots; perennial plants will reshoot.
  - Boaz allowed Ruth to "dip her piece of bread in the vinegar" (Ruth 2:14) as a condiment.

- Chapter 15, <u>Montreal</u>. Wikipedia, the free encyclopedia at http://en.wikipedia.org/wiki/Montreal.

  - Samuel de Champlain established a fur-trading post on the Island of Montreal in 1611.
  - The trading post was at the confluence of the Petite and the St. Lawrence Rivers.
  - In 1639 a Roman Catholic mission was established there with the primary purpose of evangelizing natives.
  - In the center of the city is the three-headed hill called Mont-Royal.
  - On its south is the St. Lawrence River.
  - Ville-Marie was also the center of trading furs in Quebec.
  - The Mohawk Indians lived near Ville-Marie.

- Chapters 15 and 18, <u>Medieval French Literature</u>. Found at http://en.wikipedia.org/wiki/Medieval_French_literature.

  - *The Fifteen Joys of Marriage* was published between 1480 and 1490.
  - It was a riotous critique of wives.
  - It also provided an accurate description of family life in France in the 15th century.
  - It was attributed to Antoine de la Sale and Gilles Bellemère, the bishop of Avignon.
  - *The Farce of Master Pierre Pathelin* (English) was a

popular play in its day. It was written in 1465. Its author is unknown.

- Chapter 21, <u>Merrimack River</u>. Wikipedia, the free encyclopedia at http://en.wikipedia.org/wiki/Merrimack_River.

  - The Pemigewasset River merges with the Winnipesaukee River at Franklin, New Hampshire, to form the Merrimack River.
  - The Merrimack River flows past Concord, Manchester, and Nashua, New Hampshire.
  - The Merrimack River takes a northeast bend at Lowell, Massachusetts.
  - It then continues past Lawrence and Haverhill, Massachusetts.
  - It enters the Atlantic by Newburyport, near Boston, Massachusetts.
  - Its tributaries include
    - the Souhegan River, which extends west from the town of Merrimack, New Hampshire;
    - the Nashua River, which flows north into the city of Nashua, New Hampshire;
    - the Concord River, which flows north from Concord, Massachusetts, to Lowell, Massachusetts; and
    - the Shawsheen River, which also flows north and joins the Merrimack at Lawrence, Massachusetts.

- Chapter 21, <u>Algonquin Indians</u>. Wikipedia, the free encyclopedia at http://en.wikipedia.org/wiki/Merrimack_River.

  - The Agawam Indians dwelled on the lower reaches of the Merrimack.
  - The Pawtucket Indians dwelled at Lowell, Massachusetts.
  - The Nashua, Souhegan, and Namoskeag Indians dwelled around Manchester, New Hampshire.
  - The Pennacook Indians dwelled northward from Bow, New Hampshire.
  - The Winnepisseogee Indians dwelled at the source of Lake Winnipesaukee in New Hampshire.
  - They were all members of a nation of Algonquian speakers known as Nipmuck.

- Chapter 24, <u>History of Canada</u>. Found at http://en.wikipedia.org.wiki/History-of-Canada.

  - The French explorer Jacques Cartier noticed the presence of a thousand Basque boats fishing for cod fish.
  - Inexpensive salt was available in Europe in the early 17th century. This made it economical for almost anyone to fish and resell the cod weeks or months later in European markets.
  - Cod, like a few other kinds of fish, is non-oily and was sprinkled with salt and dried to preserve it.

Nonfiction by

DAVID E. PLANTE with LORRAINE M. PLANTE

KIDS DON'T BUILD BOATS

DAVID E. PLANTE
with
LORRAINE M. PLANTE

Nonfiction by

DAVID E. PLANTE with LORRAINE M. PLANTE

CPSIA information can be obtained at www.ICGtesting.com
Printed in the USA
LVOW062322220113

316711LV00004B/284/P